I0823561

THE OLD MAN BY THE SEA

ALSO BY

DOMENICO STARNONE

Trick
Trust
Ties
The House on Via Gemito
The Mortal and Immortal Life of the Girl from Milan

Domenico Starnone

THE OLD MAN BY THE SEA

Translated from the Italian
by Oonagh Stransky

Europa editions

Europa Editions
27 Union Square West, Suite 302
New York NY 10003
www.europaeditions.com
info@europaeditions.com

First publication 2025 by Europa Editions

Translated by Oonagh Stransky
Original title: *Il vecchio al mare*

Library of Congress Cataloging in Publication Data is available
ISBN 979-8-88966-130-6

Starnone, Domenico
The Old Man by the Sea

Cover design and illustration by Ginevra Rapisardi

Prepress by Grafica Punto Print – Rome

Printed in the USA

THE OLD MAN BY THE SEA

1.

I was on my way to the beach, having slept poorly the night before due to the strong wind. How quickly the weather worsens here, taking its toll on my back, knees, everything. The sea was loud and rough, scattered shreds of blue sky dotted the water's surface, pursued by dark clouds. I kept my hat pressed to my head with my left hand and held onto the railing of the wooden steps that cut down the dune with my right, I carried a folding chair over one shoulder and had my beach bag slung across my chest. I was lost in thought, walking along when suddenly everything stopped: the wind and waves, the grasses and shrubs, the beating of my heart, my blinking eyes, the thrum of the rusty barbed wire fence that cordons off the private properties to both the left and right. I felt confused, out of sorts, maybe I was unwell again, and in that moment of disoriented stillness, the only thing that moved was a small figure outlined in gold: it wasn't a body, a whirlwind of dust, or a flash of light, but a presence, and it ran past me down the steps and burrowed into the sand a little further on. I know exactly what that is, I said to myself, and I might even know its name, even if it doesn't yet have one.

Then everything went back to the way it was: the wind picked up, the waves went back to pounding the shore in foamy strips, the barbed wire fence started to thrum again, the grasses and shrubs bent this way and that as if wiping my sweaty brow. I started to cough and couldn't stop. I made my way down the remainder of the steps panting, crossed the beach, and stopped a few meters from where the sand turned black with water. I tried to unfold my chair but, as usual, it got stuck; to use both hands, I had to remove my hat before the wind tore it from my head and set my sandals on top of it so it wouldn't blow away, I freed myself of my beach bag. Bending over and grumbling with irritation and anxiety, I finally managed to set up the chair so that it was facing the sea, into the wind. But just as I was picking up my hat, the chair tipped over, and in that moment of peevish frustration, it happened again: I saw the sparkling gold figurine dash by the water's edge, skirting the more invasive tongues of water with agility.

Then I did something foolish. Maybe because its first sudden appearance had devastated me, I decided to react: I chased that tiny living copper thread of a caprice as if I could actually run, as if I could actually catch it. Blame it on my debilitated state of mind. I surged forward in a way that I imagined powerful but actually my right leg lifted off the ground only ever so slightly—half as much as I would have liked—and the left one, well, it's not even worth mentioning. I managed to take three or four awkward and irregular steps, but as soon as I felt the full mass of my body and noticed the agility with which the little figurine flitted off into the morning fog, towards the dark stripe of the pier, towards a young woman and a boy who may have been gathering seashells, I felt ridiculous. With my heart beating wildly and my longish hair falling into my eyes, I made my way back to the chair, bag, and hat. It felt like any drop of life I had left had been sucked out of my chest the way you siphon gas out of a canister through a rubber tube.

Easy does it, I told myself. I rubbed the big toe on my right foot; it's been hurting for some time now, the nail has turned black, I'm slowly losing it. I sighed deeply, took my notebook out of my bag, pressed my hat firmly back down on my head and wrote about what had just happened, without paying any further notice to the sea or to how the sand, blown in by the hot wind, burnished my ankles.

2.

It's hard to say how long I kept at it. I must have fallen asleep because at one point, I barely managed to grab my notebook and pencil before the tide took hold of them and dragged them out to sea.

I find this sudden dozing off, so typical of elderly people, revolting. How much did I sleep? One minute? Ten? The wind has dropped, there's the lightest of breezes, the sky has turned whitish, a shiny metallic strip stretches along the waterline. I flip through my sandy notebook, skim over what I've written. I tried to unite the two incidents from about an hour ago, to patch them together on the page along with the dunes, the shrubs, the beach and the pale blubbery jellyfish that roll in and out on the gently breaking waves. In cases like this, it helps to measure out time. First, I had the little figurine dart out of the sand and then disappear; then I tried to find a reason for her second appearance, for chasing her along the border of the wet and dry sand. But my mind and hand were both limp, and I couldn't express what had really happened. Actually, I both know and don't know what really happened; the one thing that's certain is that the figurine scared me, it sapped my energy. Maybe I should focus on that vague area of knowing and not knowing—the space where the word *figurine* is merely a palliative against fear—maybe that's what I should try and write about. But it's hard, it would take energy and conviction, not this wavering feebleness that keeps fading into sleep.

Once these tiny intrusions used to happen more frequently. Back when Nina still loved me, she referred to them as daydreams or fantasies. Laura, meanwhile, called them the crazies: you've got the crazies, she'd say, which was the same word she used to describe the cat when he zoomed around the house. They used to make Nora anxious: we need to talk to a doctor, you're scaring me, you're losing your mind. But I always wanted to keep these moments of instability to myself, for better or worse it felt like the real world was shuddering just for me. When I was younger, I used to give myself all sorts of airs. Dare to be different, I'd say. Stand out, utilize both the good and the bad inside you, be the *I* that you are, separate yourself from *them*, fuck the collective *we*, and hurry up about it, you blowhard, take the leap, see how far you can push yourself, stick your neck out. And I've received my share of dents. But time passes, listlessness increases, the body becomes less receptive, less bold, reality itself grows murky. Who would ever have imagined a surprise attack this morning? There was something downright tectonic about that fleeting figurine, I was caught off guard. And then there was that feeling of malaise: I felt like my fourteen-month-old granddaughter, Licia, who goes pale the moment her mother leaves the room. She doesn't cry but she wants to be held, she leans out of my arms so that I carry her from room to room so she can look for her mother, and when my daughter finally does return, at first the child ignores her and then she explodes with joy, kissing her mouth, eagerly biting her finger or her knee with her little teeth. Better off ignoring these sudden rifts in reality, I'm in bad shape, I feel an emptiness here at the nape of my neck, and I have no one to kiss or bite. Better off—I think to myself while sharpening my pencil—writing about the fishermen, just a few sentences, the dark shapes of their footprints in the sand, the way they set up their rods and check their lines, the cruel pleasure of catching life on a hook. Better off trying to give meaning to that fat man in a flowered shirt and Bermuda shorts who's wending his way through the mastic trees, hunting for buried treasure in the sand, skimming its surface with a rudimentary metal detector. Better off focusing on that woman—I recognize her despite the distance—walking with her eyes downcast, lost in who knows what thoughts, probably on her way back from the café near the pier.

3.

This lady usually wakes up earlier than I do. Around half past seven, when I head off to the café for breakfast, she—sixty-ish, with an attractive gait, dyed blonde hair, and pleasant features, discreetly touched up—is already on her way there, either striding through the cold waves to firm up her thighs, or strolling along the shore, dripping wet. Sometimes when I reach the café, she's already ordering her cappuccino from the friendly, young, Tunisian barman, who either reaches out to touch her necklace and tells her how nice it looks on her or gently caresses her hand. I've always liked people who playfully touch each other while talking, blending harmless desire with amusement. The older woman and younger man make a good looking couple; she teases him loudly, he so softly it's hard to hear. I observe them subtly while having my coffee at a table, so they don't notice me, then I walk the two kilometers back to my folding chair at the water's edge.

This morning, though, because of what happened, I didn't go to the café. And now from my chair I see the woman on her way back, walking slowly along the shore. When she reaches me, she stops.

"Did you see?" she says familiarly, as if we've known each other a long time, while pointing at the waterline.

I stand up and look where she is pointing: a long black line extends along the wet sand. I bend over, hands on my knees, legs open wide, to examine it. Miniscule insects cling to each other like beads on a necklace. Many of them are dead, some flap yellowish wings without taking flight. I pull myself back upright.

"Probably crushed by a wave," I say.

"All in a row like that?"

"Maybe they were dancing, celebrating their tenth day of life."

She laughs with some hesitation. "Why their tenth?"

"Just because; I doubt they live for more than two weeks."

"So little?"

"Or so much, depending on how you look at it."

These are the first words I've exchanged with someone since I arrived—excluding things like: *how much for that, I'll take a hundred grams, thank you, excuse me*—and it feels good, the woman is pleasantly expansive. We walk a little ways together, feet in the water, and she talks and talks. She talks about the October weather, how it feels like the beach is entirely hers. She talks about the fog in the distance and says it might—hopefully—be the sign of an oncoming storm. She talks about how much she loves her early morning walk, home-to-café, and café-home, three kilometers there, three back, after which she showers and sometimes even goes back to bed because—she says with a laugh—at night, when she's lying next to her husband—she laughs often, every ten words or so—she's so unhappy that she can't sleep. She goes on for a long time, making ironic comments about marriage, mentioning a little boy, Niní, who is seven and very dear to her, and criticizing her only daughter, who has decided not to give her any grandchildren and who lives in Holland. Then her register changes.

"I've been watching you, actually. I want to be honest. I've been spying on you for a couple of days now. You cut quite a figure, even in your shorts and a polo shirt."

"Actually, I have a limp and my hip is acting up, which makes it hard to sleep."

"Aches and pains don't count, my dear. What counts is your joie de vivre."

"Even my joie de vivre has a limp."

"It might limp, but at least it's still there."

"You're right."

She waves me away with her hand as if she's shooing a fly, feigning regret; when men agree with her it means that she's talking too much. No, no, not at all, I say, keep talking, it's a pleasure to listen to you. She nods, yes, she saw straight away that I was someone who knew how to listen, rare goods, the total opposite of Silvestro, talking with him is like talking to a wall. We go on like this for a bit, she hurt, me conciliating, until I say, "I'm guessing Silvestro is your husband."

"Yes, that's right."

"Husbands don't count; their ears are worn out."

"You said it. And not just their ears, everything else too. Oh, what a delightful meeting this has been."

I agree and confess that I haven't spoken to anyone for days, not even on my cell phone. I compliment her on her affable manner, her outgoing disposition, and her youthful energy.

"How old do you think I am?" she asks smugly.

"Fifty?"

"Sixty-one. I'm telling you because, on principle, I don't believe in hiding my age. What counts is good health and the ability to feel passion for something. Do you have any special passions? What do you do in life? You look like a judge; I've seen you on TV, haven't I? Yes, I'm sure of it."

I don't want to let her down. "Judge on the Court of Appeals, but I've been retired for twelve years."

"Twelve? How can that be?"

"I'm eighty-two."

"That's impossible."

She's so pleased with my appearance and my position as a retired judge who was once on television that, when we reach the path that leads between the dunes back to her house, she hesitates, wishing she could learn more about me and further our acquaintance. She's the kind of person who manages to convince themself, every single day, that they're happy, at ease in the world, a little brash, and then goes to great lengths to appear that way. If I were to reveal that for the past fifty years I've been earning a living by writing short stories and novels, we'd both feel awkward: I've always been a little embarrassed about my line of work and she's probably never read any of my books. I prefer to let her talk, she's eager to show me her earrings, she touches them gently, making them sway from her lobes. She lost one, she informs me, somewhere right around here, last May, and she was so upset that a friend—well, friend is a big word, a decent person—went to great lengths to help her find it, and even succeeded. But he didn't find it straight away, no, not even a day or week or month later. No, this friend found the missing earring just a couple of days ago—isn't that incredible?—five long months after she lost it.

"Never despair," I say.

"Exactly. And you know what? When he handed it to me, I literally cried for joy."

"I bet the earring cried for joy, too."

"Now you're teasing me."

"Not in the least. Objects get attached to us, too. They despair just like we do if we lose them."

"Silvestro would never say something like that."

"Maybe because it's stupid."

"Or maybe because only a sensitive person would think like that."

She doesn't want to leave without telling me that her name is Evelina—I'm Nico, I say—and that she owns a clothes shop in town, but not cheap stuff, not rags, she clarifies, pretty things that have been crafted by the best tailors in Italy and across Europe. I say goodbye—ciao, Evelina, have a good day—and return to my chair with a twinge of regret. Discovering that she owns a boutique was an unexpected gift. I wish I had told her, with just the right dose of melancholy: you know, women's apparel has fascinated me ever since I was a child; if it's no trouble, I'd like to come see you; I'd like nothing more than to sit in a corner and admire the clothes, your clients, you.

4.

I spend the remainder of the morning reading *The Toilers of the Sea*. When I get bored, I close the book and do a few writing exercises. I carefully note down small movements of the body, insignificant feelings, fragments of speech. In the past they've proved useful to me, I've gotten details, gestures, and mutterings out of them.

When I write like this, I always use a pencil and eraser. As a boy, I enjoyed seeing the twisted gray particles accumulate on the page, they smelled good, I erased often and eagerly. Now they disgust me, I brush them away with the flat of my hand, often I don't even bother erasing. If up until two or three years ago, I wrote with maniacal precision, searching high and low for lively ways of expressing what I saw unfolding in my mind's eye, relying on my eraser if I didn't manage to capture it the first time around, now, even before I start writing, words seem artificial, metaphors seem presumptuous. Nonetheless, I scribble away for hours without second thoughts. I promise myself that later on I'll go back and erase things (*the sand, blown in by the hot wind, burnished my ankles*, for God's sake, *burnished*, it's so true that the older you get, the worse you write), but I already know that I'll forget. It feels like when things get written down they lose substance—the fishermen, their rods, the jellyfish, the strip of insects, the lost objects and their weeping, Evelina—and this at first vexes me and then, incongruously, makes me feel lighter, as if I had suddenly managed to slough off some pointless anxiety.

In the meantime, the sea has turned dark, pasty, the waves look like long white fissures, the wind has picked up. My stay here—for the past thirteen days I've been living in a house on the dunes—has been full of sudden fluctuations in light, color, and mood. Now, for example, I feel revived, the waves look like purple tar, bubbling up and over the breakwater. Colors chase and crash into each other. A fuchsia-colored dog dashes off to the right, barking. A girl appears from the left, she must be twenty or so, she's dragging a red canoe towards the water, the rope digs into the skin of her suntanned shoulder, the wind blows her blue sundress against her small breasts and belly.

Sundress: what a beautiful shiny word; my mother used to wear a light blue one that she sewed for herself. She made everything she wore with her own two hands, she was a dressmaker. For a few months in 1954, she even had a shop, which she called her *butík*. But she made more clothes for herself than for her clients, and she knew how to make herself look far more beautiful than any of the women who paid her to make them look good. Even when she had to go out to buy bread or fruit, she'd walk out of our low-income building looking like a rich movie actress, like a different mother entirely, whether she had on her winter coat with its astrakhan collar, or a pencil skirt, or a bell skirt, or her sundress. And maybe she actually was a different woman, that's how I see her now anyway, my eyeglasses briny with the sea air, my nerves shot, cataracts clouding my sight. When she went in the water, she'd never go in deep and she always swam the breast stroke: her long neck extended, her chin held high, her mouth closed so as not to swallow the salt water, her small ears with their delicate lobes. She often lost things on the beach that she considered precious, and when she started digging desperately in the sand, we children would always try and help.

Naturally, I know that the girl dragging the canoe is wearing a different kind of sundress than my mother's. Actually, on closer inspection, it's not even a sundress: it's a blue two-piece outfit. I'm just applying an ever-more uncertain fragment of memory onto the figure of the young woman with her canoe. And it's fine, it makes me feel better, I let the fuchsia dog scamper about and watch the girl as she pushes her craft into the water, hops in, and immediately faces the oncoming waves with strong, elegant strokes of her paddle. My mother, well, she never rowed a thing in her life; at most, she may have come out in a rental boat with me, when I was sixteen and she was thirty-five, how tan she used to get. All the same, I pretend, just for a few seconds, that the young woman in the canoe—who I suddenly realize I've seen around—is her, the woman who will eventually bring me into the world.

I do it, I admit, on bated breath. For decades now, I've been conjuring up my mother and putting her in places where she is not and could never be—on the ledge of a building at dawn, or looking down from the landing of a house we used to live in—it's easy enough to do. But this is the first time that I have ever irradiated her out, melded her—both verbs are wrong, or maybe it's the syntax, I'll have to think about it some more, find other words or construct the sentence differently—onto a body that has nothing to do with hers, except for the fact that she's more or less the same age my mother was when my father fell in love with her, loved her, lived her voice and breath not for how they really were but for how he hoped they were, even feared they would be. And in the years that followed, she—she, she, she—ended up feeling molded, hammered, and shaped by her husband's outbursts of rage—where are you going, who are you seeing, why are you dressed like that, you don't understand the shit that goes through the head of men, how they only think about fucking—until she gave in and resigned herself to becoming the receptacle for all his fears and suspicions, none of which were ever confirmed and which tormented him constantly; or maybe she got dressed up so elegantly and attractively to strike fear into him, to humiliate him, and in so doing, get revenge.

For a short spell my mother is part of both the canoe and the girl, but she seems on edge, scared, and so do I. So, using my imagination in a more controlled manner, I delicately place her on a strip of sunlight that crosses the water. Now the only person in the red craft is the girl, and she heads towards the horizon with easy determination, as if the sea were calm and not churning noisily. Her movements look so powerful and deliberate to me—me, with my feeble gestures, the lids of my eyes so weak that I can't even keep them from closing, not to mention open wide—that she seems ready for the impossible. Her paddle strikes the water cleanly, she appears and disappears amidst the waves, I can't follow her, she's already far away.

5.

The thread of light fades. I decide to stand up, move around, I want to learn the language of canoeing, the mere thought brings me joy. So, the following day I walk into town and look for a sporting goods store. I find one not far from the pier, its interiors are blue, decorated to look like a deep-sea submersible. I walk in with some embarrassment. I've never done sports, only walking, a lot of that, but I've spent most of my time sitting down. And that's exactly what I say to the salesman—*I've spent most of my time sitting down*—and then I explain that I'd like to learn everything there is to know about canoes, that I envy people who know how make them glide across the surface of the water.

"You should get a kayak. Why bother with a canoe?" he says.

"Canoe, kayak—I know nothing."

"To be entirely honest, I see you better in a kayak."

"Maybe, I don't know," I reply. "First I'd like to learn the language: the names of the materials they're made of, their sizes, prices, things like that. Buying a kayak, without knowing anything about them, seems a little reckless at my age, I've got no muscles to speak of, even the word kayak feels heavy, and I definitely don't see myself dragging it out to the beach every day."

"But you're not in bad shape."

"I'm eighty-two."

"So? What's eighty-two these days? Think of when you'll be a hundred and twenty. Get out there and enjoy a kayak; there are some amazing lightweight ones on the market. Have you done any research on internet?"

"No, I don't trust it."

"Bravo. Human contact is always better."

The man pulls out some catalogs and shows me all sorts of crafts in a wide range of colors: white, gray, green, green and gray, gray and white; hard shell kayaks, modular ones, inflatable, single, tandem. Finally he pitches me a single, ultralight, four-meter-long kayak that, my good sir, has a price tag of nine hundred and fifty euro but which I will sell to you for nine hundred.

"Does it tip over easily?"

"Of course not."

"Because I'm afraid of drowning."

"You know how to swim, don't you?"

"Yes, but I haven't swum for years. And if water gets in my ears, I can't hear for weeks."

The shop owner draws me deeper into conversation. He has a handsome face and raven hair without a single strand of gray; his small, dark blue eyes flash maliciously, his voice is hypnotic. I begin to get bored only when he takes my arm in a familiar manner one too many times, constantly repeating his pitch, which has since grown old. I'm about to cut him short when I see the girl from the beach walk by the shop.

It looks like she's about to come in but then she reconsiders and stops to look at the window display. The shopkeeper notices her and interrupts what he's saying about the virtues of kayaks to call out hello. The girl nods coldly and walks on.

The man smiles to himself as if I weren't there, then snaps out of it, and goes back to singing the praises of the craft with reinvigorated power of persuasion. For nine hundred, he'll throw in a double-acting pump, a waterproof backpack, a paddle, and an airtight container for my cell phone. I glance at my watch and promise to come back soon. I walk out just in time to catch sight of the girl, she's far off, a tiny dot at the end of the main street.

I follow her, feeling like my father when he stood on the bridge of the switching yard and caught sight of my mother walking on the street below. She was delivering an order of gloves and he rushed down the grassy berm, came up behind her, and asked if he could walk with her a bit; she glanced at him quickly and said no, you're too old, even though my future father was born in 1917 and she in 1921, so, really, they were only four years apart. And here we are, I think to myself, I carry so much of my father in my body that now I'm following you, with roughly sixty years difference between us, let's see what I can make happen.

The girl reaches a shop with a large plate glass window, pulls up the security gate, and disappears inside.

6.

I stand on the threshold. "Can I have a look around?"

"Sure."

I walk through the shop, admiring dress after dress, until I find one that I like—green with tiny yellow flowers. I lift the hanger off the rack and hold it out in front of me as far as I can.

"Could you show me how it looks on you?" I ask the salesgirl without actually looking at her.

"Sure," she says again.

The girl takes the hanger from me, removes the dress, holds it up to herself, and looks at me politely. Clearly she didn't understand. So, while glancing meaningfully at a mirrored nook with a wine-red curtain gathered to one side, which had to be a changing room, I ask, "Would you be so kind as to try it on?"

Her expression changes. I read something in her eyes that says: try it on? Now that's a bit much. "Is it for your wife?"

"My mother," I say, and she looks at me with alarm, probably thinking: this old man's mother is still alive, and he wants to buy a hundred-year-old woman a flimsy, practically transparent dress with a plunging neckline, now, at summer's end, and, just to be sure he's not wasting his money, he's asking me—a twenty-year-old girl—to try it on for him?

"This dress is not suitable for an elderly woman," she says seriously and with a hint of hostility.

"You're probably right," I reply. "But would you try it on anyway?"

"Sorry, but the owner doesn't want that."

I stare at the dress that she continues to distractedly hold up to her body. "Fine. How much is it?"

She says the price, it's excessively high, maybe she thinks that I'll try and negotiate, but I don't care. I don't even blink. As she's wrapping up my purchase, I go back to admiring the dresses, touching them lightly, lifting the hem of a blue skirt out to one side.

"Have you changed your mind?" she asks cautiously.

I don't reply, and besides, she asked softly, as if not to disturb me. She's less casual than I imagined, on the beach she seemed more determined, but maybe that was because of the effort she put into dragging the canoe down the beach. Once she's done wrapping up the dress and tying the package with a red ribbon, I step away from the racks and hand her my credit card. As soon as she realizes that everything is proceeding smoothly, she regrets her earlier suspicions, grows congenial, and says: the sea is so nice at this time of year. Then she softly adds one more thing. "If your mother doesn't like the dress, it's not a problem, just remember to keep the receipt."

I nod—she has no idea that I'll definitely be back—and walk towards the door, stop, peer closely at the mannequins' dresses, and step out into the street. She probably thinks that I regret my choice, that I want to have a closer look at some of the dresses in the shop window from the outside, and only starts to worry when she sees me walking away.

She runs to the door but I'm already halfway across the piazza when I hear her voice calling out, "Signore, your package!"

I don't stop, I just raise my arm and wave back, as if to say don't worry about it.

"Your package," she says, echoing herself.

"It's for your trouble," I say loudly without turning around.

7.

I wait for her on the beach, I know she'll come back. But three days go by and there's no sign of her. Finally, on the fourth day, she shows up a little before two o'clock; she gets to the bottom of the steps, strips down to her bathing suit, and drags the canoe into the water. I observe her discreetly, she doesn't even glance in my direction. And why on earth should she? Why should a twenty-year-old girl notice an old man who's either reading, writing, or dozing off and then waking with a start? Soon enough she and her boat are a dark spot on the horizon.

It's hot, so I decide to go for a swim. Walking cautiously, I make my way from the hot sand to the water's edge. My big toe with the blackened and loose nail aches. I'm careful not to step on one of the wasps that lay dying on the wet sand. Once I'm in the water, I'm scared of jostling a warty crab, treading on a spider fish, or rubbing up against a jellyfish.

I swim a bit of breaststroke, then stop and tread water for a bit. I look at the sky, at the empty beach, and then at the sea around me, also empty, now that the canoe has evaporated. But I can't stay long, soon I'm chilly, and when I walk out of the water, clouds cover the sun. I'm freezing cold—my feet, my belly, my chest—but luckily I brought my robe with me in my beach bag.

I'm shivering when I put it on, and so I pull the hood up over my head. My oldest daughter, Elisa, gave it to me about fifteen years ago; actually, it was her mother, whom she addresses by her first name, who chose it and bought it for me. I remember how she said, "Nina swore that your favorite color is brown," as if to underscore the fact that I left her when she was young, that everything she knows about me comes from her mother. When I eventually unwrapped the gift, she laughed joylessly and said, "It's too big, it's too long, you'll look like one of Magnasco's monks." And it's true: I look like a gnarled, old, gaunt monk. All that's missing is a rope belt. But I don't mind. Actually, I've come to love this burnt Siena robe; it might be old and worn out, but I don't want to part with it. It's one of the few gifts I've received from Nina and Elisa together, mother and daughter; the result of their way of hating me for abandoning them and for appreciating how I continued to take care of them, while still keeping them at bay. I really ought to focus on—I think to myself while striding up and down the shore to get warm—this fear I have of hurting people, the way I try and avoid getting hurt, and, incongruously, how I always manage to push people away and make them stop loving me, as if it were my right.

Once I feel warm again, I stare out at sea. The black dot that is the girl in her boat is growing larger, but it looks like it's happening too fast, as if the wings on her paddle were those of an oarsman from beyond the grave. In actual fact, a warm wind has started to blow, and the canoe looks like it's flying across the surface of the water. I could carry on with the image of the oarsman and say that the capable young rower is returning from the underworld with all the female shades of my life, but that would be too facile. None of the women I have ever loved—and especially Nina—had anything in common with my mother, not her hair color, expressions, features, gestures, or her tone of voice. I fled from my mother, I avoided using her as a basis for comparison, even this girl doesn't resemble her at all. But I can't deny that something has happened, that something is happening, and now here she is, back on land, dragging the boat up on shore, and finally she looks at me.

Since the hood of my robe is still pulled up over my head, I figure she won't recognize me. But she does, and she even waves to me as if to prove it. I remain indifferent and look beyond her, I stare at the sea behind her: I don't want to wave back, it would be a wasted gesture. And so the salesgirl is embarrassed, she looks almost worried, and she stops looking in my direction altogether. Dripping wet, she drags the canoe back to the steps, where she chains it to a pillar, throws on some clothes, and hurries off, maybe to reopen the shop.

I observe her out of the corner of my eye, the way I did with my mother, both when I was young and older. I never wanted her to see me watching, I always hoped to learn her secrets when she was distracted.

8.

I stayed on the beach longer than usual, the afternoon slipping slowly into evening. At one point, as the man with the metal detector was walking past, behind me, his instrument beeped. He immediately crouched down and started digging in the sand. He's very fat, so when I see him on the beach and watch how he moves, I always feel a little sad.

"Find anything?" I asked. He didn't reply so I tried again, this time more politely. "Did you build that yourself?"

He got to his feet with a sigh but with more spring in his step than I expected, given his bulk, and kicked at the pale sand.

"It's not against the law," he said.

"No, I don't think it is, and even if it were, the last thing I'd do is call the police."

This didn't pacify him, actually he walked off muttering to himself: police, judges, you're always breaking our balls.

I figured he was a friend of Evelina's, in small towns like this, word gets around fast. She probably said: you know that old man on the beach, the one that rented the condo on the dunes? Well, he's a judge, a famous retired magistrate, he used to be a judge on the Court of Appeals. And so it goes with gossip, inanities that travel from one person to the next. It's all my fault really, I can never be bothered to contradict someone and explain how things really stand, so I tend to agree: yes, I'm a banker, a professor of classical philology, I sell insurance, as well as reassurance, I'm a barkeep, a cruel man, a holy friar who's been dunked into hot tar up to his bellybutton, a golden aureole suspended over his head. Sometimes I mispronounce my last name the way my interlocutor does—for crying out loud, I shouldn't talk to anyone anymore, not even myself.

I looked closely at the man's thick calves, the dark puddles of his footsteps, the ring of light sand around the uneven brown circle that he dug with his hands and feet. I called out to him. "My mother lost a gold necklace, one earring, and her wedding band on the beach."

"Did she lose her husband too?" he asked with surprising irony and without looking up.

"No, just the jewels."

Often, people wriggle away when I buttonhole them. But sometimes they grow curious, and a dialogue is born. That's what happened with this man. He hesitated, behaving as if he had found something in a tangled cluster of clam shells, plastic bottles, and driftwood, but truthfully he just wanted to see where the words would lead, he hadn't really found anything. But I had, and to see better, to make sure it wasn't an illusion, I pulled myself up out of my chair with a groan. Yes, I had seen well despite having cataracts in both eyes, which I've chosen not to operate. While digging in the sand, the man had actually unearthed a small treasure, but since he was only interested in the beeping of the machine and precious metals, he hadn't noticed the bill: a fifty euro banknote was sticking out of the sand.

"Signore!" I called out. "Look! You found something." He glanced at me suspiciously and waited for me to walk over. I waved the money at him. "You found fifty euros."

"No, you did," he said, addressing me with the familiar *tu* form.

"No, you did," I insisted, likewise shifting to the informal voice.

"Not at all; I didn't see it."

"But would I have seen the money if you hadn't dug up the sand?"

"No."

"And so . . . "

I've always thought the moment when mistrust flips to trust, and then into friendship, to be beautiful. Because of his weight, the man's face was large and hostile, but suddenly his eyes were full of mirth. We chatted a bit about good luck and soon I realized that he was well-educated: one path leads to good fortune, another to misfortune, we stand at the crossroads of life, destiny, fate, the Parcae, etc. etc. I then tried to convince him that he really had been lucky: if, at the sound of the beeping, he had stopped five centimeters away and dug up a different pile of sand, the bill would have remained buried forever, or the tide would have swept it away. He hesitated for a moment and then said that he had been lucky not because of the money, but because he had walked by me—I must have looked like some kind of holy man in my brown robe—and not some scumbag crook, of which there are so many.

"We'll split it," he said gruffly, slapping my arm with his outsized fingers.

"No, that would be stealing. It's yours."

"Then I'll help you look for your mother's gold."

"That's kind of you, but impossible."

"Why?"

"Because it didn't happen here."

"Where then?"

"In a small town called Scauri."

"That's only a few kilometers away."

"True, but it happened a long time ago."

"No problem. I've found stuff that's been buried under the sand for years. A friend of mine lost an earring while she was walking to the café one day, and guess who found it, even though several months had passed? Me. It takes patience and method."

I looked with renewed interest at the treasure hunter. "In addition to patience and method, you also need one of those contraptions. Did you build it yourself?"

"Yes."

"Are you an engineer?"

"No. You all think that if a person has studied Tasso's *Dialogues* or the collected works of Leopardi, they can't possibly understand electricity. I used to teach literature, but even so, I know how to assemble a tool like this."

"Clichés help people live easy."

"And stay stupid."

He then went on to bray against local political parties, the town leaders, the State, viruses, the threat of nuclear war, the rise of neo-fascists in Italy and around the globe, how liberals are shifting right, drought and floods, the diffusion of inhumanity, the decline of schools, how ignorant and inefficient his ex-colleagues were.

"Why ex?"

"They fired me."

"What did you do?"

"I fell out of favor."

"With the administration?"

"With everyone."

"Why?"

"I was odious."

It's always painful to see a man humiliate himself by saying something like I'm odious, and I told him as much. He snickered but in an ugly way, with his mouth closed, as if he was afraid of showing his teeth, and insisted that even if his intentions had been good, he always expressed himself poorly, taking the wrong tone, making it easy for people to hate him. "They can't have fired you just for that."

"Well, they did."

"What line of work are you in now?"

"I'm not."

I thrust the fifty euro bill at him and this time he took it but in exchange he wanted me to take the metal detector.

"You deserve this and more," he insisted. "You're kind. I saw tears come to your eyes when I told you they fired me."

I hadn't realized it but it was certainly possible: old age has made my nerves fragile, and my eyes well up at hardly anything. "You don't fire a teacher just because he's odious."

He sneered unpleasantly. "Why not?"

9.

The dunes at night are anything but silent. The sea gasps, the sand moans, the scrub puffs and pants, the air drips with moisture, both indoors and out. Generally I sleep deeply for two or three hours and then wake up. But one night I sleep for only about an hour, the room is hot, my cell phone says it's twenty past one. I try to empty my mind of thoughts but sleep is not easily deceived. Fine, I say, let's get up and look for some kind of temporary distraction.

I climb the stairs that lead onto the terrace but I'm annoyed by the damp railing, the slippery steps, the ache in my big toe, which makes me feel even more unsteady on my feet, and by the mosquitoes and millions of other flying or still or slithering creatures attracted to the light that I'm forced to switch on so I don't fall.

It's cold outdoors. Soon enough, I start to cough and the aches and pains in my knee, hip, and shoulder all increase. From the darkness beyond comes a tornado of tortured noises, all living matter is coming to blows, I can hear the ferocious and frightened screams. I'm disturbed by how, at times, the line that separates me from everything else thins out, I fear it will snap, and especially at night. The sound of the sea and the smells that fill the air make my head spin. I go back inside and make my way listlessly downstairs, almost falling two or three times.

I stare at myself in the bathroom mirror. My eyes are murky and foul, my irises seem rotten. Behind me, in the corner, I notice the metal detector that Maurizio, the ex-teacher, lent me. He insisted that I keep it for a few days; have a little fun with it, he said as he was leaving. I propped it up next to the vacuum cleaner, now I risk confusing the two. I stare at it while yawning loudly and repeatedly, producing a long sound that I immediately wrote down: uaaargh, which is more meaningful than my previous *The sea gasps, the sand moans, the scrub puffs and pants*. Actually, I yawn so widely that I pull something, a painful knot forms under my chin. Am I tired or bored? I don't know. By now it's probably three o'clock, an hour when things lose their shape, even I feel progressively more indefinite. There's no moon—I go check—only a few streaks of light, a couple of stars, the night air over the sea is as dark as the tip of a well-sharpened pencil, I just can't stop this frenetic insomnia. I grab the metal detector and a flashlight and head to the wooden steps that lead down to the beach. The painful knot under my chin suddenly disappears, I face the sand. I want to tire myself out with Maurizio's machine.

Flashlight off, I advance with the necessary caution, letting the metal detector explore the sand. I step on seashells, crab claws, spiky twigs. Before I was hot, now I'm cold. The device is heavy, it doesn't beep. Maybe I'm not using it correctly, or maybe what I think I'm looking for has gone to great lengths not to be found. At this time of night, I shouldn't be wondering where the gold-edged form might be hiding, I know full well that it makes no sense to look for her with a device designed for finding metal. You're such an idiot, I tell myself: you couldn't even come up with a sentence to hold her still on the page for a second, and yet here you are in the dark, thinking you'll find her with this rudimentary tool, your teeth chattering, your feet sluggish and numb with cold. Still I keep at it. I like this walking, blindly and slowly, flanked on one side by the noise of the sea, the small waves breaking on the shore, only their pale crests visible. In its pointlessness it is narratable. And all my life I have done everything, literally everything, to satisfy this mad desire for story.

I walk for about half a kilometer before realizing I'm not cold anymore. I'm sweating now, I'm scared of getting pneumonia, and I'm just about to turn around when I hear a man's voice. I think I hear him say, loudly but warmly and persuasively: there's no harm in it. His words are followed by a woman speaking harshly: you've got to stop harassing me. I switch off the metal detector and stand still. The man and woman discuss something for a moment but it's hard to make out what they're saying. They might be walking away, occasionally it sounds like the woman is crying. Her tears sound fake but now the man is upset, he raises his voice: enough, I can't stand this anymore.

I should turn on the flashlight, I think, but not so I can see them, just so that they know I'm here. I do it—no one's in front of me. I shine the light to the left, in the direction of the dunes. I see an elegantly dressed man in a light-colored blazer and dark trousers but no woman. For a second I wonder if maybe he had been doing both voices, one deep and the other in falsetto, as if, while out walking at night, he had recalled an argument, an old lover's tiff, as if the words and sobs had slipped out of his memory through his mouth. The sense of propriety that made me turn on the flashlight now compels me to turn it off. I think I recognize him, it might be the owner of the sporting goods store where I went to ask about a kayak. But my eyesight is ruined, and besides, the shop owner didn't seem like the kind of man who'd be wandering up and down the beach in the middle of the night. I turn on Maurizio's contraption and head slowly back to the house, my legs heavier than usual. I can't hear the man anymore, but then I feel a dark shadow run past, sobbing, and the metal detector beeps.

Should I turn the flashlight on? Keep it off?

I quickly switch it on then off, making it wink like an eye. The metal detector beeps repeatedly.

I turn the flashlight back on and look down at the sand. Money, again: four one hundred euro bills held together with what looks like a gold money clip.

Time for bed.

10.

I woke up in an excellent mood. While shaving with the usual care, I even started singing *oimarίoimarίquannusuón-naggiupiérzpetté*, but soon stopped to avoid nicking myself. I walked into town, even though the sky promised rain—I like rain, never see it as a threat—and I detest driving. Not a drop fell and it was very hot. The sky was dirty white with one long dark cloud that ran through it like a shard of rock.

I arrived at Evelina's boutique, saw her standing behind the counter, busily doing something or other, and I walked in. Here I am, I said taking off my hat to make sure she recognized me. At first she looked startled but then her eyes lit up.

"Nico," she exclaimed. "What a wonderful surprise, come in, sit down."

A yellow settee and pair of bright green boudoir chairs were arranged in the corner: they were small and far too colorful. Last time, when I had bought the dress, I hadn't noticed the furnishings. The salesgirl's presence had erased everything unconnected to our conversation and my purchase. Now things were different. Evelina doesn't command as much physical strength as her employee, and I even less. As a result, we are at risk of being overwhelmed by the setting, it may come to count more than we do. So I mentally banished the display of accessories—bracelets, earrings, necklaces, scarves—as well as the white walls, standing mirrors, the crowd of autumn dresses on their hangers, two elegantly-clothed mannequins, a blue glass table, an ashlar vase filled with blood-red gladiolas, a silver bowl overflowing with gelée candies, how dull. Instead I forced myself to focus entirely on Evelina, who was gesturing for me to sit down, having already hung up my sweaty jacket and Borsalino.

"How lovely," she said in a slightly hoarse voice. "I have a wonderful assistant, who unfortunately is often late, but as soon as she arrives, I'll have her make us some coffee—and you'll see, it's even better than the one from the café."

I glanced around. "What a lovely shop, such creative furnishings and elegant clothes."

"I'm glad you like it."

"I've always been fascinated by *butíks*. My mother often used that word, she thought it was so evocative, she was a dressmaker."

"Oh really, a dressmaker."

"Yes, very creative, and extremely beautiful. I'd love to spend a little time here, just sitting quietly in a corner, breathing in the smell of new clothes."

Evelina looked so enthusiastic it was as if I had confided a great secret in her. "And why shouldn't you? Come whenever you want, stay as long as you like, I can't believe that you want to spend a little time with me."

"I don't want to bother you."

"Are you joking? How could you possibly bother me? It would be a pleasure."

Then she took one of my hands in hers, squeezed it tightly, and kept talking with excessive warmth: to have you here, with me, well, I'd do anything, anything at all, really. It felt nice to have my hand held so gently, it showed me exactly what kind of woman Evelina was, the kind I'm comfortable with instantly. They hide their discomforts, troubles, or embarrassments from others and themselves, and if they do end up talking about such things, they do it with affected amusement, making it hard to discern their true thoughts and feelings; actually, the more intensely painful their secrets are, the more they cluck and chirp and giggle seductively—ooh, thank you, Nico, thank you, I feel the clouds lifting, it's going to be a good day after all.

When the shop door opened, she slowly released my hand and benevolently scolded her assistant: Lu, finally! I turned to look, triggering a sharp pain at the nape of my neck. Obviously, Lu was the girl with the canoe, and as she walked in Evelina tapped the face of her watch with her index finger: punctuality, my dear, we've been waiting for you for thirty minutes, hurry up now, and make us some coffee.

When the shopgirl caught sight of me, her color faded from beautiful gold to drab gray, and she greeted me with some hesitation; I quickly realized that my surprise appearance, sitting on the settee with her boss, was embarrassing and maybe even a little worrisome, so I replied warmly to her salutation. "Good morning, Lu. And thank you again for everything you did last time; you were a great help."

Evelina did not appreciate the fact that we had already met. "You know each other?" she asked with a scowl.

"I bought a dress the other day," I said.

"The green one with yellow flowers," Lu interrupted me to add.

"Right," I went on. "And this young lady gave me some excellent advice."

Evelina went back to speaking gaily, complimenting me on the choice—such a chic dress, she had picked it up in Paris—and going on to say that if any tailoring was needed, she had a workshop, the dress could be taken in, let out, shortened, anything at all. Even so, I detected in her voice a hint of bother at the fact that I had women in my life for whom I bought dresses.

I said and did nothing to quell her concern; in that instant I was only concerned with making sure Lu didn't feel vulnerable. She must not have told her boss—I was now certain of it—that I had left the dress behind as a gift for her, and she was probably worried that I would mention it, or even worse, that I had come back for it. I turned to Evelina: the dress is perfect, I said. Then I looked back at the girl: you really gave me excellent advice. And while speaking, I looked at her warmly and complicitly, and her golden color returned; I'll make the coffee now, she murmured, and disappeared through a door in the back of the shop.

At that point, I focused entirely on Evelina. I contrived a vaporous story about how the bodies of certain living people remind us of our dead, how our dead live on through the living, fusing and confusing and diffusing, irradiating past into present, death into life, life in death, essentially saying: I have a granddaughter who reminds me exactly of my mother, and I bought the dress with yellow flowers for her.

Lu came back in just as I was telling the lie but showed no interest in what I was saying. I took a sip of the coffee—delicious—and Evelina, once again happy with herself and the world, went back to praising her sales assistant. She's like a daughter to me, so capable, priceless for dealing with my foreign clients, she speaks three languages, English, French, German, and even a bit of Russian, we used to get a lot of Russians before the pandemic, before the war, we did good business with them, but there aren't that many around anymore. And to top it off, she's beautiful—Evelina added in that tone of voice that women use when they're drawn to the beauty of other women—look at her shoulders, Lu, show the gentleman your muscles, she's made of rock, she is, she could beat you at arm wrestling in two seconds flat.

Nodding ever so slightly and with a hint of a smile, Lu chose not to show me her muscles.

"Well, I'd better be going," I said.

"Oh, no you don't; now you're behaving worse than my husband, making all sorts of promises and then not carrying through."

"What did I promise?"

"That you would stay."

I was about to reply and say fine, I'll gladly stay a little longer, when something must have happened out on the street, behind me. Evelina's eyes lit up, she forgot all about me, and she turned to Lu.

"Well, would you look who's here," she said.

Lu turned to see. "It's the second time he's skipped school this week," she said softly.

Evelina got to her feet, excused herself, and went to the door. Curious to see, I turned around, but slowly and carefully because of my stiff neck. Standing outside was a boy with a backpack. Seven, maybe eight years old.

"Get in here, you troublemaker, and give me a kiss." Evelina opened her arms wide and leaned over, the child ran into the shop and the safe warm harbor of her embrace, and energetically kissed her on the cheek near her mouth.

"You can't stay here," Lu said. "Go to your father's house."

"He's asleep."

"Wake him up."

Evelina picked up the child, held him tightly to her

chest, and then started to scold him playfully. "Why aren't you at school?"

"They didn't let me in."

"Liar," Lu interrupted him. "Where have you been until now?"

"On the beach."

Lu looked out the window and said to the child: you're not allowed to go to the beach on your own. Then she turned to Evelina: look, Dr. Martano is here. Then to Niní: let go of Evelina, we have to work now. I turned around to look out into the street again. A petite and heavily tanned woman was crossing the piazza towards the shop, she was tiny even though she had on very high heels, which she wore with great skill. Excuse me, Lu said, and I stepped aside, making room for her to quickly clear away the tray and coffee cups.

What to do: take my leave despite Evelina's invitation, or stay? I suddenly felt very awkward. My mother used to close the bedroom door when her client, the stunning signorina Pagnano, took off the clothes that she arrived in to try on the outfits that my mother sewed for her and admire herself in the mirror. I knew I was in the way and yet I stuck around; I could still feel my mother's hand at the nape of my neck, on my upper back, delicately pushing me out, then shutting the door. I am like Niní is now, or maybe even younger, only four or five, but not as cute or nice as he is, an annoying child, the kind that adults automatically dislike even though they're good and obedient, the kind that adults are embarrassed to admit they detest. Even now, sometimes, I suddenly feel out of place like that, the wind drops out of my sails, words fail me.

"So why didn't you go to school?" I asked the boy.

He didn't reply.

"Did you have something better to do?"

Niní looked at me carefully.

"I went to look for the sea monster."

"There's a sea monster out there?"

"Yup."

"Who told you?"

"Papà. But he says it's only in our heads."

"What do you think?"

"I don't agree."

Evelina squeezed him tightly and said that sea monsters don't exist, not in our heads or anywhere else for that matter.

"What kind of monster exactly?" I asked. "A giant squid?"

Niní nodded but with some hesitation.

"With four hundred suckers?"

Niní nodded a little more confidently and gave a slight smile.

"What will you do if you find it?" I asked.

"I'll follow it home, then kill it."

"Do you have a boat?"

"Yes."

"What's it like?"

"Red. Do you have one?"

"No, but I'm going to buy one."

Evelina put Niní down. "Are you really sure you have to leave?" she asked with regret, but less keenly than before.

"Yes, but we'll see each other again soon."

"I'm counting on it. Don't disappoint me."

When I got to the door, I stood to one side so the small

graceful lady could enter, bringing with her a pleasant whiff of perfume. "Good morning, Dr. Martano," I said.

Perplexed, Dr. Martano looked at me, and off I went.

11.

No rain, the white clouds had fled and gotten tangled in the mountains, the sky was clearing. A strong wind must have blown because the road was full of broken branches, pine needles, dead leaves, geranium petals, and rotten oleander blossoms. I didn't feel like going home so I did a little shopping—fruit, mainly—and then walked to the sporting goods store, which wasn't far away. Not for the kayak, I admit, but the owner. I wanted to hear the sound of his voice and was even tempted to playfully ask: so, what were you up to last night on the beach near my house? But he was busy. He stood off to one side in that submersible-themed shop, with its fake portholes and various shades of blue, talking to a big-breasted woman with red hair who spoke a foreigner's Italian.

"I'll be right with you," he said politely.

"Take your time."

And that's exactly what he did. He and the woman carried on an intense conversation for at least ten minutes. They spoke in restrained tones, articulating their words softly so that only the other could hear, and not me. From where I stood, it seemed like the woman was annoyed, angry even, she kept opening her mouth as if to take a bite out of him, then snapping it shut. He, on the other hand, spoke warmly, suavely; he kept repeating her name—Irmtraud, the sound and its exoticism reached me clearly, Irmtraud,

Irmtraud—with some difficulty and yet with gusto. At one point he grazed one of her deeply bronzed arms with his fingers. She pulled away but not immediately, only long enough to revel in the contact before remembering either her anger or my presence, an embarrassing witness.

I pretended to examine fishing rods, neoprene wetsuits, a beach chair made of some kind of very flexible steel that looked especially comfortable, while simultaneously gauging the voice of the shop owner. I had ruled out that he was the man on the beach, but not entirely. Since he seemed shiftier than most other human beings, it occurred to me that it would be hard to transcribe him onto the page. While he was well-built and even rather handsome, there was something else about him. What was it? When he accompanied the redhead to the door, for example, his tone of voice changed a little, and he started to speak—or pretended to speak—in a tone that veered towards a falsetto, as if he was talking not to a woman but a child. This man has all sorts of mimetic capabilities, I said to myself; he plays himself like an instrument, and he does it well, competently and imaginatively. Yes, it probably was him out on the beach last night. As for the woman, it's harder to say; she didn't seem upset now. As she walked out—probably because she had managed to obtain what she wanted from him, at least temporarily, raising her spirits—she teased him for wearing too much cologne and even caressed his cheek.

The shopkeeper watched her walk away under the noonday sun, turned around and—either because he was pleased with himself or to see me waiting for him—cheerfully and emphatically clapped his hands hard, once, and rubbed his palms together multiple times. "Have we come to a decision, my dear sir? Do we want this truly splendid kayak?"

"No," I said. "I still have some doubts. To begin with, I read that the best kayaks are hard shell ones, not the inflatable kinds. And then there's the problem of carrying it down to the water, its upkeep, inflating and deflating it—how will I manage?"

The shop owner took me seriously, far more than I took myself, and did everything he could to reassure me. As he was probably the kind of man who derived energy and confidence from each "yes" he managed to coax out of the ladies, and since he must have recently obtained, by feigning defeat, some kind of consent from the red-haired woman, he started to string together sentences with gleeful arrogance. When he suggested a product to a client, he explained, he always tailored it to the person who stood before him. While it was true that hard shell kayaks were better performing, of course they were, what did a man like me, at my age, want to do with a kayak: slalom racing? The craft he had suggested was better suited to my strengths; yes, it was inflatable, but it was the best model on the market, a perfect boat, it could handle all conditions, and it was resistant. He would deliver it to me himself, and with regards to the rest, well—he said—take a walk down the pier. You know how many people you'll find who'll gladly inflate the kayak for you and bring it to where you're sitting on the beach for just a couple of euros? They're better than robots—he said enthusiastically—which are just machines after all, and programmed to grow obsolete, soon they start giving you problems and then, one day, they quit working altogether. From there, he went off on a tangent and tried to convince me that there's no more efficient and trustworthy machine than a hungry human being. Following that, he started in on a paean to slavery, which had been stupidly substituted by salaried work, he said. And where has that led us? Slavery—he explained—was a tested system; you crucified those who rebelled and everyone else behaved for centuries. Meanwhile, my dear sir, just think of the troubles that salaried workers have brought us. Also, how do we know that machines won't one day destroy us? Do you go to the movies? Do you listen to the experts on TV? Slaves are stupid; or else they wouldn't be slaves. But machines? They're always getting smarter. You, clearly, are an important man—he said emphatically—and you'll have to admit that the great men of history would've remained minor figures, and that poetry, art, and science would've remained dreams, if there hadn't been people to dress and undress us, to shave us and trim our nails. But now we're becoming so stupid that we're even considering depriving ourselves of that useful final vestige that is a servant?

I interrupted him—You can't be serious!—but I said it without hostility and even smiled as if it were obvious that he was joking. And in fact, he looked down at the ground and snickered politely, as if to say: you almost fell for it, didn't you? Then he looked me straight in the eyes and with great amusement said that—seeing how cyborgs still weren't available for purchase, but when they were, I would definitely be able to find them in his shop—I could rest easy and buy the kayak because I had already found the perfect slave, the person who would take care of all my problems: him. In other words, he would be at my service 24/7, and if he were sick or too busy, well, he'd be sure to send a trustworthy and capable individual so that I wouldn't find myself saying for God's sake, now who's going to carry my kayak down to the water for me?

He carried on a while longer and I stood there listening, trying to memorize the words he used as if I was still a young man and had all the time in the world to try to get all the stupid things he was saying into writing. But then I got bored.

"What's your name?" I demanded brusquely.

He was momentarily disoriented and replied with some uncertainty, as if he couldn't quite remember.

"Silvestro."

"I don't want to waste any more of your time, Silvestro. I trust you. I'll buy the inflatable kayak."

He was silent for a moment before congratulating me. "Bravo, well done. I'm glad you'll be able to enjoy some time out on the water, under the open sky. After all, there's no denying that summer is here to stay."

"But I'll pay you eight hundred euros for it. I don't need the waterproof backpack or the airtight case for my smartphone. I barely use my phone on land, and definitely won't bring it with me out on the water."

"Impossible. The best I can do is eight-fifty, but even then I'll be losing money. You'll have to pay for the pump and the paddle."

"Fine for eight hundred fifty, but with the pump and paddle."

He accepted, bringing the niceties to an end. "You'll pay in cash, I hope."

"I don't have cash."

"You can go to the ATM machine."

"Sorry, but I'm half-blind; I have a hard time entering my pin number."

This disgruntled him even further, and with some resentment he accepted my card for payment. But as soon as he recalled that he had ripped me off, overcharging me at the end of the season for a kayak that had probably been sitting in a warehouse for a long time, his good mood returned, and he started talking about how dissatisfying it was to use credit cards, how much more pleasurable it was on a tactile level to count out fifty-euro or hundred-euro banknotes. Just think, even pussy—he said with smug vulgarity—even pussy, my dear friend, will one day be electronic, fingers and cocks will fall into disuse and atrophy. At the mere thought of that mutation, his blue eyes blazed purple with pretend bitterness and malice, and then he began to roar with laughter, showing off his large, bright white teeth.

At that point I felt the need to get as far away from him as possible, the same way I had felt when I was nineteen and had a temporary job in a middle school office, where I was constantly tormented by the head secretary, a peevish woman in her late-fifties, and well-liked by a male colleague who was around forty, a man who was always well-dressed and clean shaven, whose pretty wife sometimes came to see him with their two daughters, aged three and five.

In addition to being proper and polite, this colleague often tried to shift the head secretary's ill-will for me onto himself. But then, a few days before my temporary position was up, he, who was usually so composed, showed a level of discomposure that shocked me to my core. Taking advantage of a brief absence of the head secretary, the man leapt up from his desk, walked straight over to mine, and set down a plastic reproduction of the female genitalia—complete with vulva, mons pubis, large lips, small lips, and clitoris—while hissing like the snake in Eden:

nice, right? You like it, right? Without waiting for a reply, he then hurried back to his desk where he recomposed himself. For the rest of my time there, for all the hours and days I had left in that office, he'd look over at me and wink and smile, and even though I had come to detest him, even though he frightened me, I couldn't not show small signs of complicity. If men like that had ever buzzed around my mother, my father would have killed them—and I might have, too—first them, and then her; he always said that she was too trusting, that she never thought about the consequences.

What a man's world it had been sixty years ago. And Silvestro? How old was he, I wondered. Fifty? Fifty-five? I rule out the possibility that he's carrying around a vulva made of plastic or some other material in his pocket. But I have no doubt that he'd gladly share any number of photos or videos with me from his phone. I know too much about people like him, I could write a detailed history about this type of virile male, so I spoke up loudly and interrupted him. "When will you bring me the vessel?"

He looked at me as if I had spoken in a foreign language. "The vessel? Oh, I'll have to ask the warehouse about the vessel—a week, more or less."

"Out of the question. I gave you eight hundred fifty euros and you want to deliver it in a week?"

"Four days, possibly. Would four days be alright? What's the rush?"

"There's a giant squid out there," I say somberly.

He looks at me, relaxes, and laughs loudly.

"And, at eighty-two years old, you want to go hunt for a giant squid in a kayak? Do you have a slingshot? Or you want me to find you one?"

I remain serious. "I don't need a slingshot. To kill a squid, you need to cut off its head."

He slaps me amicably on the back.

"What line of work were you in? Were you an actor? I know I've seen your face before. You're very funny, your comedic timing is perfect, I'd gladly spend the day with you."

"I'd definitely advise against it. I've written and performed humorous things before, but it's been a long time since I've actually made people laugh."

12.

I didn't sleep well again last night, I had a nightmare. I dreamed that at dawn I walked up to the terrace and looked down with compassion at bodies of women that the sea had washed up on the beach. Many of them were still alive. I was awed by how they struggled, first to get onto their knees and then to pull themselves up to standing. The most determined of them made their way towards the reeds in dripping wet and torn clothes, disappeared momentarily, and then reappeared as if they had discovered the source of life growing among the rushes, grabbed a handful of it, and swallowed it like a pill. I hurried down the wooden steps to follow one of the women at a safe distance. With great effort, she crawled up the dune, glanced around, and eventually squatted down to pick wild lotuses, but not in an elegant way. She ripped them out of the sand one by one, and took giant bites out of them; then she picked some more and made a sheaf with them, and hurried off to share them with the others. I picked up one of the lotuses that she had dropped, chewed on it for a while, and immediately felt much better. Even the women on the shore were regaining their strength. I watched as some of them bent down and pressed their thumbs into the skin around their ankles to see if it left a mark, and if it did they cried out: Oh no, my ankles are swollen, it's uric acid, I can't pee. Others began to dig frenetically into their own bodies, scooping out wet sand full of red worms. I hurried back to the house and went to sleep; when I woke up I was a woman.

I lay there, half-awake half-asleep, until about eleven. Now I'm going to the beach, the sun is at its zenith, the sea is calm and hot, no one's around. It's at moments like this that I have a hard time keeping my balance. The light is blindingly bright. At the top of the wooden steps, I rub my eyes to wake myself up, but my eyelids close too slowly and by mistake I touch my eyeball and hurt myself. The funereal border of insects has long gone, now the waterline is rimmed with a long necklace of metallic fragments, dashes of dark sand followed by silvery bits that shimmer in the sunlight. Panting under the weight of my habitual baggage, I set up my chair not far from the water, then go and look. They're not bits of metal as I initially thought. They're anchovies, some of them float on their sides, glistening with reflected light. I walk into the water, up to my knees. Dense schools of anchovies dart in front of me, cutting off my path, they look like ice being chipped away by a warm current. Instead, it's the swift energy of life that casts death off to one side as it passes by, fragments of animated matter rotting in the sunlight, looking like silver.

I return to my folding chair unhappy, I remove my hat and wipe my sweaty brow with my forearm. What an incongruous simile: pairing the milling of living things to metal and ice; I just don't know how to do it anymore, maybe I never did. Until 1960, I wrote just for the sake of writing, however it came to me. Then I read Thomas Mann, and then Marcel Proust, and I started to think that I needed to write in a far more complicated manner if I wanted to achieve any kind of greatness. To see what I became in those years, all it would take is a glance at a page from my notebooks, luckily I've thrown them away: long, elaborate sentences, words added merely to thicken the soup, especially adverbs and adjectives; metaphor after metaphor, simile after simile. I'd read some Musil, then try and write like Musil. I'd read some Kafka, then try and write like Kafka. I'd read some Svevo, then try and write like Svevo. Finally, after reading over everything I wrote, I would say miserably to myself: Thomas, Marcel, Italo, Franz, why did I ever read you? Look how you've ruined me. I missed the way I used to write, fresh and green again, elemental, the way I did when my teacher had complimented me, back in middle school, seeing who knows what kind of promise of greatness in it.

I should've been content with my childhood babble instead of constantly aiming higher and higher, only to breathlessly discover that, as hard as I tried, I'd only end up an imitator of imitators. Even as a young man, I found myself longing for the long threads of words that came easily to me as a teenager, and today I long for them even more fervently, while listlessly going on about wild lotuses, women, anchovies, the way death resembles silver.

I erase, rewrite, glance at my watch. I'm waiting for Lu, it's that time of day. In the meantime, I eat some grapes, I get up and walk along the shore, I spit the seeds into the water while being careful not to tread on the rotting fish. My hip and back ache terribly, my right knee hurts, not to mention my loose toenail. How I wish I could take a running start and jump high and jump far. Instead I have nightmares, I wake up tired, I struggle to come up with a single thought that helps me bounce back. Maybe I should've brought out Maurizio's metal detector, it would've taken my mind off things. It would've been strange—I think to myself—if the metal detector had started beeping near the silvery anchovies. That really would constitute an aesthetic revolution; I'd finally have proof that rhetorical figures, those curlicues that live inside my head, actually do exist, and that the silver of the anchovies, even as it decomposes in the sunlight, or rather precisely because it knows itself to be rotting silver, would reveal itself to be actual matter, with its own laws, just like the wild lotuses in my early morning dream revealed their hidden properties: eat them and you become woman.

13.

Just as I'm about to go get the metal detector—if not gold or silver, I might find more cash, I seem to be on a lucky streak as far as that's concerned—Lu shows up. Before seeing her, I hear her sandals on the wooden stairs then I look over and see her skipping down them, wearing the flouncy green dress with yellow flowers. Before advancing onto the sand, she removes her sandals and leaves them on the last step. She doesn't go directly to the pillar where the canoe is locked up, she doesn't take off her dress; instead she retrieves the paddle from a hiding place in the green brush and walks barefoot across the beach towards me. Her beauty is hers and hers alone, she clearly has no intention of breaking it up and sharing it with the sand, the scrub, the sea, my mother, me. I'm tempted to leave her to her own destiny, get up and go to the pier, see if the café is still open since high season has ended. Instead, I stay.

"Hello," she says.

"Hello."

"See?"

"Yes."

"How does it look on me?"

"Not bad at all."

"Are you disappointed?"

"No."

"Are you sure?"

I shouldn't have said *not bad at all*, I should've said *amazing*. I wish I could correct myself but it's too late. A tall, young man in a bathing suit is coming down the steps, one at a time; his long skinny legs make his balance seem precarious, he has a slender chest, and he's carrying a hiker's backpack. Lu doesn't seem to care to hear any reassurance I might offer: after asking *Are you sure?* she got distracted, now she turns to look at the young man.

"Don't tell him about the dress," she says with a little smile. "He'd be upset to find out that a man I don't know bought it for me."

"But I didn't buy it for you."

She frowns. "But it's mine now, right?"

"Of course."

The young man goes to the cement pillar, unchains the canoe and, with surprising energy, he raises the craft up over his head. He takes long strides in our direction—the canoe looking like an eccentric red hat on his head—and sets it down in the water. Lu waves him over while informing me that he's her boyfriend. The young man approaches a little shyly, he has a genuine smile.

"This gentleman is a friend of Evelina's," Lu says, indicating me. "He's a famous magistrate on TV."

"Nico," I say, introducing myself.

"Gino," he says and shakes my hand so vigorously it hurts. "Nice to meet you."

"Nico graduated from university last month," Lu says proudly.

"What did you study?"

"Engineering," Gino says, freeing himself of his backpack.

"He's really smart," Lu says, even more proudly.

"Oh, come on . . . I didn't enjoy a single class."

"Then why did you study engineering?" I ask.

"My father is an engineer, my uncle is an engineer, and my grandfather was one, too. We have a construction company and there's a lot of building going on around here."

Lu opens the backpack, takes out a towel, and spreads it out on the sand.

"If you could be anything, what would you be?" I ask Gino.

"A school teacher."

"Liar," Lu interrupts him to say, taking off her dress and revealing her bikini. "He wants to write novels, tell him how you want to be a writer."

"You can always find time and a way to write," I lie.

The young man shakes his head, he doesn't believe me, but he goes back to the other topic. "I wish I could've been a teacher. Who knows, I may still become one."

Lu disapproves and shakes her head skeptically, then,

after brushing some sand off the towel, she folds her dress up neatly and sets it down next to their backpack.

"Would you mind watching . . . ?" she asks.

I have a hard time understanding exactly what or whom she wants me to watch. There's nobody on the beach who poses a threat to their possessions; I enjoy thinking that she may have asked me to watch them as they push the boat out into the water. And despite the fact that my eyes are veiled over with cataracts, that's exactly what I try to do, and I feel good: the colors are bright, the smell of the green shrubs on the dunes and the scent of the sea blend together pleasantly, I like this Gino fellow, and I write him down in my head. Tall and skinny, he tries hard to be liked but he doesn't like himself. And so, before others have a chance to refuse him, he refuses himself; in the name of what he imagines he will become, he denies what he already is, timidly offering up a shadow of himself that he thinks is more likable than his own flesh and bones. But he constantly makes mistakes, he'll make mistakes his whole life, large and small, he'll always put off becoming the person he believes he truly is, even when it seems like it has finally happened. Others, meanwhile, will prove to be more capable than he, the women he'll love will fall for his rivals and critics—strong, sensitive, intelligent men—and they'll go on to invent subterfuges so that they feel far more appreciated by those men than he ever will be able to make them feel.

Yes, that's how Gino will be, and I like him. He has already climbed into the canoe, but then it dawns on him that he should be doing what Lu is: pushing the boat out into deeper water. The water is already up to her chest, Gino is flustered, he'd like to hop out and get into the water himself, he's made a mistake. But Lu laughs, stops him, gives one last energetic push to the canoe, and then hops into the craft so easily it's as if the sea lifts up her lithe body. Gino begins to paddle hard and eagerly, he tries to be that determined and capable young man taking the woman he loves out to sea, ready to die for her should danger appear, be it in the form of a shark or a giant squid. She lets him, but soon enough the boat slows down and comes to a standstill. My mother always showed warm displeasure whenever my father, an artist with his head in the clouds, tried to do practical things. She was tactfully skeptical about me, too: you two need to come to terms with the fact—she used to say—that there are certain things that you're just not cut out for. Some of her uncles and cousins had certain capabilities, even my brothers, but the two of us—father and firstborn son—did not. I imagine Lu is now saying something like that to her boyfriend, and I expect that the young man will obstinately insist and start paddling again, as my father would have done angrily, while me, I'm not so sure. But Gino acquiesces; clearly, he wants to see her happy and do what she knows how to do well, what she enjoys doing. And in fact, as soon as Lu takes hold of the paddle, the canoe cuts like scissors straight through the fabric of water.

14.

They disappear beyond the black outline of the pier and are gone for less than an hour. When they return they look happy, they thank me for guarding their things, then Lu checks the time on her cell phone, it's late, she has to rush back to the shop. With her towel wrapped around her, she takes off her bikini, steps into her underwear, slips the dress over her head, then drops the towel. If my mother ever did something like that—it occurs to me—around other men, even old men like myself, my father would have killed her. Gino doesn't even notice, he puts on his backpack, lifts up the canoe, says goodbye and walks off. Lu turns to me.

"Evelina asked me to tell you, if I ran into you, that tomorrow is a good day to drop by, a few of her friends are coming to do some shopping, she'll expect you at ten."

She says it reluctantly, as if she'd been deeply tempted not to relay the message. I try to look pleased to have received the invitation and promise to be there, but things fluctuate: for a while I'm sad, then cheerful, then dejected, then hopeful. I'd like to watch Lu walk off in the green and yellow dress, but I stop myself and go back to examining the anchovies along the waterline.

The silver is tarnishing, the metal of the metaphor is decomposing. Seagull prints in the sand look sarcastic, mocking. Chasing after such beauty and elegance at the age of eighty-two, with a mind like a sieve, nausea from constantly feeling like I'm going to fall over the edge, is utter foolishness. I sit back down in my chair and write. If only, three decades ago, I had found the words to describe my mother, Rosa D'Alessandro, the way the poet Giorgio Caproni wrote about his, Anna Picchi. I've tried endless times over the years and wish I could say that I succeeded, even in part. I wanted to set Rosa to the rhythm of Anna, but in prose form; because either you know how to write poetry or you sound ridiculous. But even in prose, my mother was hard to pin down. What had I managed to preserve of her? Her laughter: bright white teeth and dark skin. Or the time

I saw her crying. Or the time at the hospital when she said: I know I'm about to die. Everything else exists inside my father's words; when I was a boy, I believed his invented stories about her and never paid any mind to how she tried to invent her own life. He was extremely intelligent, an artist but forced to work for the railroad, he spoke Italian well, not just dialect, and he knew many foreign languages; my mother only knew how to cut and sew blouses—she worked from home—that were commissioned by a pretty blond foreign-looking lady with freckles, who in turn worked for a man with pitch black hair and a mustache. The two of them formed an odd couple: the pretty lady had a child and the man with the mustache had fathered many, they were lovers, she was his concubine, words my father used, initially sketching Rosa into the background, a small figure with her needle and thread, then dragging her into the foreground, guilty for having laughed too hard in that man's presence. Was she being drawn down that twisted and sinful path?—my father would scream at her—was she really and truly tempted by the clandestine pleasures that foul man promised, merely by looking at her?

The man with the dark hair and his blond lover came to our house often. He was actually the one who paid my mother for her piecework; he had an old brown leather wallet that he kept in his back pocket, and when he pulled it out, that container of wealth seemed enormous to me. Even his eyes, which shone brightly out of deep purplish hollows, were enormous; his lips seemed to be made from some kind of sticky, carmine red paste. My father found him ugly, too much flesh on his skull, and he expected my mother to feel the same way, he wanted her to admit with forced sincerity that the blonde woman's lover was horrid, that the mere sight of him was revolting, that he was a good-for-nothing, a pimp, a procurer, clearly; because when a man comes into your house and pretends to be your friend, but his real goal is to seduce another man's wife so he can then screw her, well Rosa, what's a man supposed to do—kill him, kill you, kill myself?

For as long as the man came to the house with the foreign woman to pay for my mother's piecework, my father would simply scowl and make the best of a bad situation, money is money after all. But if he dared to show up alone, and while my father was at work? Then it was all up to me; I had to keep a close eye on that ugly louse and on my mother, too; I had to make sure he didn't touch her, not even with the tip of his finger, and that she didn't dare laugh. I constantly imagined—my mind was crowded with deeply distressing images, voices and shouting, like at the movies—the awful possibility, and the humiliation that would ensue were I to notice the smallest thing happen and then lack the courage to run into the kitchen, grab a pair of scissors or a knife, and kill them both.

In all likelihood, it was my own imagination that erased my mother from my mind, forcing me, to this day, to invent just about anything in order to come up with a fragment that was truly hers from my excessively frantic daydreams. Caproni, lucky man, knew how to project himself forward via the pattering of heels, flouncing and fluttering skirts, lace borders, hemstitches, the true sounds of a true mother, with basic, elementary, green rhymes. Not me; by the age of twenty, every single sentence I wrote felt like an immense burden and struggle. I tried to keep things linear, but I ended up crawling into all the cracks, looking for connections far and wide but lacking the intellectual strength to find them, only complicating things, garbling them. Even today, as an old man, I run the same risk. I start with Rosa, soon I want more Rosa, then a little more, then too much Rosa, to the extent that I lose the little bit that's true—how she giggles while she fixes her hair with both hands—and I fall into the artificial. I have to stay calm, not go overboard, let's see what tomorrow brings. And if tomorrow brings nothing, there's still time, I'll try again.

The sun, meanwhile, sinks into the water, the sky is on fire, the air slowly turns lilac. At night, the house filled with buzzing mosquitoes, I say some of Caproni's lines out loud to myself: *tu sai cosa darei /se la incontrassi per strada*. I feel a good mood coming on, settling me, filling me. If Rosa is *like* Lu, I say to myself, let's see if I can manage to get beyond *like* and actually encounter her. Before going to bed, I recount the money I found the other night and carefully examine the money clip to see if it really is gold, then jot down in my notebook: if Evelina's husband is not the same Silvestro as the Silvestro who owns the sporting goods store, that's fine, I'll change one of their names, at this point it doesn't matter which. My good mood stays with me until I fall asleep. In the morning the weather does not look promising, the sky is dark, the humidity intolerable. If it were to rain, it would come down hot.

15.

When I arrived at the shop, my shirt was soaked, luckily I had on a jacket, I hoped they wouldn't see the sweat marks. Evelina greeted me with nervous eyes, Lu with a distracted hello, as she was busy straightening up the already tidy shop. She swiftly removed a mannequin's summer clothes and dressed it in an autumn outfit, dragged a basket towards the counter, and polished a mirror.

"Sure I'm not disturbing?" I asked Evelina.

"The more time you spend with me, the less of a disturbance you are," she said firmly, adopting, without any prior warning, the informal *tu*.

Her clients, all elegantly dressed in late summer attire, arrived a few minutes later: four in all. Evelina introduced me to them in her usual excessive way—he's an important man, a famous judge on TV—and even though the ladies smiled and greeted me, I could tell they were annoyed by my presence.

I immediately realized that I knew two of them already: the diminutive Dr. Martano, whom Evelina addressed with her title while using the informal *tu*, and the red-haired lady with the foreign accent—Irmtraud—whom I had seen in Silvestro's shop when I was waiting for the kayak. Since neither gave signs of remembering me, I behaved with them as I did with the other two: a very slender woman named Melania, with white hair and a youthful face, and a statuesque lady—Sibilla—with cheekbones that protruded like tennis balls under her taut skin, broad shoulders, and hands like the blades of a fan with which she fanned herself, a giant goddess, in other words, the kind of woman who, in ancient times, was capable of both seducing and terrifying mortals.

We politely made small talk—the colors of the sea at this time of year, it's October but it feels like August, they say it will last until January—and soon enough I discovered that the clients were all affluent and sophisticated ladies who were either putting off a return to their usual cities—Melania lived in Milan—or were born and raised in other places but worked here—Sibilla was from Bologna, Irmtraud was from a small town in the Mecklenburg region—or else, as Dr. Martano, a cardiologist, proudly said: I took my first breath in this dull seaside town and it's where I want to take my last.

No one mentioned any family ties, they presented themselves as if they were childless widows or single women who'd managed to avoid both long relationships and pregnancies. But it seemed more probable to me that they considered any men they had bent to their demands as irrelevant, and children a concern that they preferred to set to one side in that particular moment.

It struck me how often they called Evelina *our poor Evelina*—we're always bothering our poor Evelina, how hard our poor Evelina will have to work this morning—while Evelina continued to smile happily, not at all seeming like a woman to be pitied. With Lu, meanwhile, they were polite but chilly, emanating—yes, that's just the right verb—the need to keep her at a distance by barely glancing at her. I supposed it was normal; after all, these were ladies with money to burn, and Lu was just a shopgirl who needed to stay in her place; if they offered her a hand, she might take an arm, as the saying goes. Or maybe I was just exaggerating for the sake of a story the sudden sparks I noticed in their eyes, the almost imperceptible twitches of repulsion in their bodies, their tones.

It seemed that the giant woman—Sibilla—was the only one to show Lu any courtesy. She was also the only one to express any interest in me.

"Evelina has played a cruel trick on you," she said. "You'll soon be terribly bored."

"No, not at all. It was my choice to be here."

"In addition to the law, are you involved in fashion?"

"My mother was a dressmaker."

Melania spoke up without looking at me, while rubbing the fabric of a brown duster between her fingers. "My mother managed a post office in Codogno but I do everything I can never to set foot in one."

"Post offices," I replied, "are places of death, with letters and postcards passing into oblivion. But ladieswear is still festive, the life of a green blouse is full of passion."

These final words seemed to trouble Dr. Martano, but not to the degree that she felt compelled to ask: full of passion—how? Instead she stopped at the word green. Staring at the brown duster that Melania was examining, her voice somewhat annoyed, she asked: why green in particular? Good question. When I write, I always include something green and I'm not entirely sure why, there's probably no good reason for it. I was just about to say as much to Dr. Martano—*probably no good reason*—when Sibilla, holding a long skirt up to her waist, cheerfully replied for me: green, red, blue, it's not a question of color or type of blouse, it's that this gentleman still likes the ladies.

I looked at her warmly, she was truly an imposing woman, and the frankness in her tone, completely devoid of perfidy, bolstered my good mood. For a moment or two I wasn't sure if I should agree or not. Did I still like women? Still, despite my age? Despite all the experiences I've had, be they brief or long or very long? Despite all the kindness, rage, upset, disparagement, fake warmth, and violence I've had to put up with? Despite my belief that the very notion of coupledom is essentially a ridiculous construct, one that breaks down too easily and leads to a slew of ugly consequences involving family, children, relatives, unhappiness, emptiness, cruelty, and horror?

"You've embarrassed him," Irmtraud said ironically, flipping through the hangers of clothes on a rack. "One doesn't ask such things."

"No, not at all, I'm not embarrassed," I quickly replied. "I do still like women, all women, and sometimes I forget myself to the extent that I say and do stupid things. But women also worry me, I've always felt this way."

While peering at a blue dress with many buttons, Dr. Martano listlessly asked, "Why do we worry you?"

"I don't know, it's a vague feeling, one that I can trace back to early childhood memories. When my mother dropped me off at preschool, I always cried, I never wanted her to leave. So all the little girls would kiss and hug me and brush my hair, and put clips and ribbons in it."

"They wanted to make you feel better," Irmtraud said tenderly, thinking of the little girls.

"Perhaps, but it only made me feel worse. I used to worry that my mother wouldn't recognize me with all those ribbons in my hair, and that she'd leave me there forever."

Dr. Martano shook her head slowly, setting aside a skirt. "You didn't trust your mother, did you?"

I looked at her strangely. No, I said loudly. As Evelina must have noticed how her friend and client's comment had disturbed me, she exclaimed to everyone: see how charming he is, so easy to talk to, after just a few minutes you feel like you can open up to him about anything. Sibilla was the only one who looked like she agreed, the others nodded distractedly, the expressions on their faces revealing how they saw me: as a dull, wrinkly, liver-spotted, droopy-eyed old Boeotian, with white hairs sprouting from my nose and ears; we barely say hello and he's already reminiscing about preschool, he's going to ruin the morning. . .

I sat down on the settee and took out my notebook and pencil, hoping to give them the impression that I wasn't an old Boeotian, and that I still had plenty of things to do.

16.

The staging was pointless; they promptly forgot about me. They turned their focus to the autumn fashions and in a matter of minutes the carefully studied shop was in total disarray.

Initially the instigator of the chaos was Melania, assisted by Evelina, who, at the slightest hint of interest from her client, expertly reached for the hanger, removed the article of clothing and held it out to her with such a light touch that it seemed like the dress had come to life. How beautifully Melania's white hair framed her delicate face. Everything about those women was lovely. Her curiosity made the others curious, her interest provoked general interest, and soon enough there was much complimenting, yearning, competing, and envy.

Poor graceful Evelina never once lost her patience and always managed to keep her client-friends in her line of sight. One moment she was encouraging Dr. Martano, the next she was flattering Sibilla, then she was raving over Irmtraud, who stood holding a dress on a hanger up to her body in front of the mirror, the curve of its hook clawing at her tanned neck, her forearm pressing the outfit into her belly, one leg lifted, as if poised to drop-kick her reflection.

It took them a long time to choose their ensembles,

but eventually each lady found dresses and blazers and dusters and trousers to try on. At that point there was a great back-and-forth to the changing rooms. Melania went in, Irmtraud came out, Dr. Martano went in, Sibilla came out. They strode towards the mirrors in the manner best suited to the ensemble: whether flared pants or narrow-legged trousers, in blazers, cardigans, and peacoats, each of them becoming less of a client and more of a model, prancing around for themselves and the others. They gesticulated with their arms and swayed their hips, but not too much, they stopped a few inches away from the mirror with their feet turned out, elbows in, the palms of their right hands extended, as if offering something on a tray.

I didn't miss a single fluttering eyelash. This is why you're here—I told myself—assimilate gestures, feelings, words; focus on the movements, colors, and sounds rather than on what they mean; what importance does meaning have now, the main thing is that something happens. For almost two hours I watched the women parade streetwear, all black oversize clothing, droopy shoulders, shocking pink ensembles, and every single outfit was—in Evelina's lexicon—rock n' roll, fabulously textured, or totally whimsical. The ladies contemplated each other, unhurriedly recognizing both their similarities and differences. They gushed—that looks so good on you, it would be awful on me, not with my body type, I could never, no, but on you it looks perfect, maybe with a chunky necklace to downplay it a bit—and languidly caressed each other, as if appreciating the feel of the fabrics on other women's bodies triggered their own need for contact. Show us! they cried over and over, putting on and taking off the autumn clothes in the late-summer warmth of the shop, reveling in the idea of wasting money and energy. The clothes grew even more alive, creating complex needs, releasing passions of all kinds, mother-sister-lover, affectionate phrases piled up: how gorgeous you are, how adorable you look, that fabric is perfect on you, so smooth, elastic, sinuous, slippery, wavy; it resonates, vibrates, trembles.

Lu, meanwhile, held an essentially servile role in the grand scheme of things, and I admit that I kept an eye on her with a little apprehension, but she held up her end. Their requests came crashing into her, faster and faster, piling up. Can you hand me that, Lu? Would you bring me this? Never calling a thing by its name or mentioning its color, just voices and commands, uttered in a range of tones: Dr. Martano was often demanding, Melania was formal but polite, Irmtraud showed studied indifference, Sibilla was cordial. The shopgirl was unflappable, focused, she never missed a beat. As soon as an arm appeared from behind one of the wine-red curtains, she knew exactly what was expected of her. She'd walk calmly to the counter and get a pair of high-waisted pants from the heap; she'd unravel a scarf from around a mannequin's neck; she scurried up the ladder and brought down a camisole. She never pronounced judgement, never showed what she thought. When, for example, Sibilla asked her for her opinion—she was the only one to do so, everyone else asked Evelina—Lu just nodded slightly, maybe it was a yes, maybe it was a no, and then looked over at her boss, who immediately chimed in with a phrase like: we can shorten it, if you want, at which point she'd say to Lu, see what you can do, and Lu would get down on her knees and start to pin up the excess fabric that pooled at the feet of Sibilla's statuesque body, who in the meantime continued to share her thoughts with Evelina, Dr. Martano, Irmtraud, and Melania.

That was a key moment for me: seeing Lu on the floor, and the ladies standing around her in fashionable clothes. Suddenly, and with acute violence, I recognized the smell of life in all that dressing and undressing, in the modelling and posing. It was the same scent that my mother's clients exuded when, seventy years earlier, they came to our house for fittings, to try on the clothes that my mother was making for them, or when Rosa measured out a dress for herself. Sure, things have changed since then—I told myself—the words we use now to describe womenswear are different; as a boy I never heard words like twill carré or denim or pea coat uttered by my mother or her clients. But what has remained, despite changes in the smell of the protective treatments, is the all-enveloping odor of a new article of clothing, how it's woven through with pleasure, with delight and anguish, because life slips away from us, it thins out, the body changes and falls apart. I recalled how that scent used to spread through and fill our small home, two rooms and a kitchen. My mother did her sewing on the table near the fireplace, there was nowhere else to do it. The table where she cut fabric, where she kept her pins and buttons and chalk and thimbles and buttons and spools of various color thread, was the same one that had to be cleared so that we could eat, a square not far from the stovetop and a step away from the corner to which she'd abruptly retreat and, hunched over, urgently start treading the pedal of her sewing machine. It was there that she served us our lunches and dinners, but despite all the cooking she must have done, I have no recollection of the smell of sauces and gravies, I remember only the smell of fabric and her excitement, which wafted down the hall to the room where I slept with my brother, the very same room where her clients tried on the clothes for their fittings during the day. It was then, after recognizing that scent, there in Evelina's shop, that Rosa appeared.

17.

But maybe the word *appeared* is excessive, I need to use more words to begin to describe what happened. It wasn't that I didn't want my mother to appear, I just didn't want that version of her—the way she was two days before she died, when she got dressed with utmost care and asked to be taken to the holy sanctuary in Portici to thank Saint Cyrus for healing her.

We all went with her to visit the saint: her five children, my father, the whole family; but my memory of that morning is a little faded, as I set it aside decades ago. However, even if the memory had been clear, the notion of an elegant but moribund mother is disruptive, I had wanted something different. But it's too late: the cream-colored foulard that she wore that day around her neck suddenly became crystalline, with the recollection of the graceful way she pulled the scarf up over her withered hair before entering the church, framing her jaundiced and puffy face, imposing itself forcefully on the scene. Nothing doing: my mother is here, in the shop, in her skirt and blazer. She must've gotten here hours ago, gripping tightly to Lu's life-filled body. The women keep chatting without noticing her, while she suffers: she's as excluded from admiring herself in the mirror as is Lu, she rubs her belly, grimaces in pain, mumbles yes, thinks no, mumbles I'm going to be sick, thinks no, impossible, mumbles I'm dying, thinks no, it can't be, I don't want to die, I won't die.

Less than six months ago, she was a beautiful young woman. Now she's shapeless, she's lost all composure. The transformation took place suddenly, cruelly. After her death, I start to fear that this abrupt decline will suddenly manifest itself in the bodies of every other person I care about: friends, lovers, children. Even I, although never actually afraid of death, will live with the fear of the way a young, healthy body can precociously break down, without having the time to adapt to the aches and pains of old age. My mother never had time to get used to, or resigned to, old age, but I have. Maybe that's why, to this day, I can't comprehend, and I'm troubled by, how two days before dying, Rosa concealed her moribund state even to herself, put on some elegant clothes, and imagined that Saint Cyrus had not only restored her good health but had also restored her beauty. Most of all, I'm disturbed by the thought that she presumes she can be here in that physical state, with her arms in her blazer ravaged by intravenous needles, kneeling in front of Sibilla like Lu is, and actually trying to push her way into the space that the girl's future-filled body occupies.

Wrong tense—I write—wrong mother, wrong Rosa, wrong shadow. My system of concordances isn't working, there's a flaw in the first term of comparison. My mother is welded to Lu, but there are no affinities between them, Lu looks uneasy, Rosa has nothing youthful or energetic about her. Even the way she expresses her affection is wrong: to let us know that she loves us, she merely smiles. The lexicon of this young mother on the verge of dying—she's only forty, my father alone knows that the doctors released her so that she could die at home—is reduced to words related to her illness: distended belly, ascites, splenic vein. This is the state in which her shadow comes to me; she reaches out from a time when she was twice the age as the shopgirl; it was October then, too, the fifth or sixth, I think. She hadn't made clothes for anyone for more than a decade, just for herself, and maybe not even those. She had lost her flair, imagination, hope, good taste; she no longer dreamed of having a boutique; she no longer had clients who wanted expensive fabrics with floral patterns or animal prints, who wore small hats decorated with feathers from exotic passerine. The ladies had grown weary of her handiwork, they'd liberated themselves of it and of her, all the dresses and blazers and skirts she'd sewed for them over the years had probably been sold at the huge second-hand market in Resina, or turned into rags for rag-sellers, into dishtowels and cloths for dusting, or used as scraps in contemporary artworks. Even so, her mind must've still been filled with the tornadoes of words from the work she had done years before. She'd been using them since she was young, and had used them with even greater frequency and referring to her own body when she was planning to lead a different life, when she still dared to hope for more, to escape from us, the men of the house, at least for a couple of hours. I relished those nouns and adjectives: taffeta, bordeaux-colored shantung silk, lace tulle, royal blue synthetic satin, white silk chiffon, or strawberry-colored with a silvery hue, *moredoré* (what is *moredoré* anyway?), bronze and purple sequins scattered across the table, organza. I learned those words by heart when I was young so as not to lose sight of her; my life was an intolerable contradiction. I liked my mother better than any other human being in the entire world: I watched her, enchanted, as she divested herself of mamma-mammà-mammì-ma' and transformed into a diva more beautiful than any of the movie stars on the Palmolive billboards. And yet, when she was making clothes for herself in the kitchen, sensational outfits that she wore with insolence, I both feared and hated her, I knew I'd only feel relief and free—free from devotion, free from the anxiety that one day she'd leave me—if she were dead.

I look at her, and it hurts. Weak as she is, on the verge of dying, she kneels down in front of Evelina's clients. She reaches out a slender arm, her pale hand delicately takes some pins from Lu's tight-lipped mouth, and she fastens the excess fabric of an oversize dress more securely to Melania's hip.

18.

"Was that boring for you?" Evelina asked me.

I said no, and it was the truth. All six of the women—for a moment there were seven, and then my dying mother coughed, the barely perceptible dry hack of discomfort and illness, after which point I no longer saw or heard her—turned to look at me, suddenly remembering my presence. All of them, except Lu, were dressed in fall clothes, even though it was still very warm. Melania wore a trench coat, Dr. Martano had donned an oversize biker's jacket that made her, short as she was, look like she'd been attacked by a ferocious beast, Sibilla flickered in pink, with Irmtraud's brown tailleur effectively muting her like darkened glass, and even Evelina had put on a tiered cornflower blue dress, as if she intended to buy her own merchandise, and now stood facing me, one foot in front of the other, hands deep in the pockets of the dress.

I looked at them with affection, they looked like they'd just stepped out of a blender in perfectly blended outfits. Around them, it was as though the Great Weaver of woven goods had erupted into a thousand pieces, the spirits of all the clothes had vanished, leaving behind splotches of color, shapeless rags draped over the counter, table, and chairs, and even on the floor.

Dr. Martano glanced at her cell phone, it must've been crowded with messages because she frowned and muttered, "It's late, I have to run."

The words *late* and *run* trilled like a bell through the room, and the ladies quickly changed back into their summer clothes. All except Evelina, who stood at the counter in the cornflower blue dress, punching numbers on her calculator, with Lu next to her, wrapping up the merchandise with mechanical diligence, her forehead shiny, her skin somewhat sallow, as if something of my mother's deathly illness had stuck to her. I felt guilty, as usual I expect too much of myself and the result is flawed. The morning seemed to have come to an end, one by one the ladies cordially came and sat down next to me on the settee. Clearly I hadn't disturbed them, maybe they now considered me someone they knew well, an acquaintance, a new kind of girlfriend who had the benefit of being a polite and elderly gentleman. One of these evenings—Melania said—we'll invite you to dinner, we'll tell you about our lives and you can tell us about yours. I'll tie colorful ribbons in your hair—Sibilla added seriously—and I'll bring my scissors: your hair's too long, too white. We were sitting there chatting when all of a sudden we were interrupted by a man's deep voice, warm and yet imperious.

"Still here? No one's hungry today?"

Instantly, the ladies forgot about me. It was Silvestro, the owner of the sporting goods store; I recognized his voice immediately, the way he intoned those few banal words. There and then, I was annoyed by his arrival, I didn't much like him—he, meanwhile, seemed thrilled to see me: you're here too! how wonderful—and although his manipulative capabilities were interesting at first, they quickly grew annoying. What surprised me was the power he held over these elegant, well-educated women. Instantly, and merely with the sound of his voice, not only did he set them all on edge, as if they were afraid of revealing something they wanted to keep hidden but which was quickly getting away from them, he also had a physical effect on each one of them. Evelina lost all luminosity, her pleasant face drooped like a faded rag. Melania ran her hands through her hair in an artificially casual manner, making a bun at the nape of her neck. Dr. Martano fiddled with her bangs as if she had suddenly lost her composure, revealing an unattractive forehead. Sibilla smoothed down her dress with her broad hands, and Irmtraud, startled, undid the top button of her shirt, as if she needed to air her generous chest. Lu, who until that moment had kept her eyes downcast, suddenly looked up with shocking boldness. In other words, it was as if a sudden gust of wind had destabilized them all, making each of them lose the pose they'd held all morning.

The tension only increased in the minutes that followed, with each gesture and short phrase signaling something that I did not know.

I kept an eye on Irmtraud as she was the only one I knew

a little bit more about. I had been present at her tête-à-tête with Silvestro—in that phony submersible, surrounded by fishing rods, wetsuits, oars, and spearguns. I observed him, his movements, how he maneuvered her by centimeters, millimeters even, until she was so close that she could lean her red head of hair on his shoulder. If I can see it, I thought to myself, then surely the others can too, particularly Evelina. But Evelina didn't seem to notice, she was busy ringing up the purchases, and on closer examination, I noticed that the other ladies weren't behaving all that differently from Irmtraud. While they may not have been seeking out her same level of physical closeness, they were entirely oblivious to the amounts they would soon have to pay and focused instead on teasing Evelina's husband with irony, giggling at his self-deprecating responses, with which he alluded to certain peccadilloes and weaknesses with shameless smuttiness, all punctuated with familiar gestures and congenial clichés.

I got up from the settee to get a better angle on the entertainment, but immediately felt ill at ease, as if I had crashed a party where everybody knows everything about everyone. Silvestro tucked a lock of Irmtraud's red hair behind her ear, put one arm around Melania's waist, and the other around Dr. Martano's shoulder; at a certain point he reached out for Sibilla and took her by the hand, as if worried she might tip over. While he appeared to be enchanted by them—he listened to them agape, staring at them with his blue eyes, leaning in as close as possible, as if he needed to feel their breath on his skin—his words were not at all kind, especially as regards Melania—Melania, you need to eat more, men need something to hold onto, you've got nothing to hold onto—always acting like a fox with sour grapes. As a result, no one was visibly offended, they laughed and almost seemed grateful for his vulgar comments combined with his fleeting caresses. Except when he cut them to the quick—which he did especially with Melania and Sibilla.

And so it went for a while. Then Silvestro, perhaps hoping to amuse the ladies even more, decided to draw me into his banter.

"You must have made our gentleman friend's head spin with all your chatter," he said, scolding the ladies. "Fluttering around him with no regard for his age. Good thing I showed up to save him. Are you trying to scare him away? You better not, he's a good client; he made a large purchase in my shop."

I gave a little smile of gratitude, and not just to play along. Without intending to, he not only had brought me back, restored me, he had also—I realized with relief—granted me the possibility of reassigning dreams, muscles, and vitality to Lu.

"Actually, I'd like to buy a few things too," I said.

Lu looked up at me first; we stared at each other for a fraction of a second.

"But, my dear friend, it's time for lunch," Silvestro exclaimed.

"It won't take long. That is, if Evelina will do me the favor."

Evelina replied without concealing that she could give fuck-all about her husband's appetite. "We can take as long as you want. What did you like?"

"To start with, the dress you have on. Do you have it in a smaller size?"

"You want to see a Small?"

"Yes," I said, motioning vaguely towards Lu. "If the

young lady could try it on, it would avoid all sorts of problems."

"Your granddaughter is Lu's size?"

"Pretty much."

Silvestro burst into laughter, with Irmtraud giggling in imitation. "So, there's a granddaughter."

Evelina glared at her husband. "Stop being stupid; he's a serious man."

Silvestro raised his hands in fake surrender. Now Sibilla laughed.

Evelina, trying to calm her angry voice, asked me to give Lu a couple of minutes, just enough time to wrap up the ladies' purchases. Let me finish with them—she practically whispered, gesturing towards her client-friends—and I'll be right with you. But the four women—even Dr. Martano, who'd said she was in a hurry and continued to receive a barrage of messages on her cell phone—suddenly discovered they could all stay a little longer—no, no, don't worry about us, you go right ahead, our new friend has already waited long enough, and besides, we want to see what he chooses—and those who had already picked up their large shopping bags printed with the shop logo set them back down on the counter. As soon as they noticed that I had returned to the settee and that Silvestro had joined me, they each looked around for their own place to sit. Irmtraud perched on the armrest next to Silvestro while Melania took the one close to me; Dr. Martano and Sibilla sat down in the two green armchairs. In the meantime, Evelina, torn between being warm with me and hostile to her husband, asked Lu to look for a Small. Lu went to look but did it slowly, wearily, or maybe her manner was intentional, carefully studied, as if we were spectators and she on stage.

They had it; the shopgirl slipped into one of the changing rooms and closed the wine-red curtain behind her.

19.

With the rustle of Lu getting undressed, the ladies practically withered, as if the happy wave of the morning had finally retreated, together with all the ironic amusement. Silvestro's joy, meanwhile, grew as if he had reached a goal far beyond his ambitions. He turned to me and murmured in my ear, but in such a way that everyone, including Evelina, could hear. "My dear friend, my wife says that you're a serious man so let us speak seriously: how old is this granddaughter of yours?"

I almost-whispered my reply. "If I told you the age of the woman I'm about to buy clothes for, you'd be very surprised."

He didn't react well, I saw in his eyes and open-mouthed expression a sudden look of intolerance. He must have decided early on that I was a decent old man, with no silly ideas in my head, *buono come il pane*, as the saying goes, but my recent comment must have led him to think that I wanted to confuse my life with his own. He seemed almost offended by the possibility but had no time to reply as Lu stepped out in the cornflower blue dress.

Her eyes were no longer those of a weary servant but shone brightly. What had she done? Pulled her hair up? Put on a little makeup to go with the dress, a hint of some miraculous lipstick? Or nothing at all—was it the dress that had given her a new shape, transformed her into a new Lu? The shopgirl was gone, gone was the athletic young woman with the canoe, even the girl who had worn the expensive green dress with yellow flowers over a blue bikini to impress her boyfriend was gone. She was another Lu, one I couldn't define, an amalgam of tangled gazes belonging to Evelina, Melania, Sibilla, Dr. Martano, Irmtraud, Silvestro, and yes, even mine, which blended and flowed through theirs.

There and then I expected Silvestro to pick up where he had left off and come out with some vulgar comment. But he sat next to me in total silence, staring at Lu. His sudden speechlessness must have disoriented the ladies. Melania, her shoulder grazing the fabric of my jacket, practically fell apart. And not just her, but everyone, even Evelina, who stood at the counter, fell into that deep cornflower blue, the rich color slid across the girl's shoulders, rose slightly over her nipples, flowed across her thighs, and gathered at her knees. The shopgirl boldly displayed just how the shape of that dress could multiply the joy of being alive. But there was something else. Lu, in that cornflower blue dress, made it perfectly clear to the women that everything about that morning spent trying on clothes had been an illusion, nothing they had felt or purchased would satisfy their need for beauty and elegance as much as once glance at her did, as the figure she cut in that shade of blue. That's when melancholy started to set in. The more the scale tipped from pleasure to delusion, the more their mood darkened, the more their irritation grew. Lu had swept back her hair in a way that accentuated her long, firm neck. She had taken off her bra. She had refreshed her eye makeup, the bitch. She had taken advantage of the fact that I, the client, old fool that I am, had asked her to try on a dress, and now it was as if she was saying: it's not my fault, I didn't do anything, he asked me to do it, the owner told me to do it, in other words throwing their affluence and good taste straight back in their faces. Lu, that invasive and cheeky girl who refused to stay in her place, had taken possession of their costly fantasies and was flaunting them indiscriminately. She even managed to undermine Silvestro's crude game of sighs and innuendoes; with just a few simple moves, she had him by the nose. She was truly splendid.

"So? What do you think?" Evelina asked me.

I shook my head, no. They were certain I would have nodded affirmatively, they were waiting for my yes so they could return home with their little sorrows. Instead I said that the size was right but that the color was wrong, the tiers were wrong, that the dress looked better on Evelina.

"What?" Dr. Martano blurted out, managing to capture the disappointment of all the women present. Even Silvestro looked at me in shock. Yes, what was I saying? Was I truly a Boeotian or, for some reason, was I lying? Lu looked so stunning that saying otherwise was stupid, you could only either envy or hate her for it; or else, you could empower her further, go beyond any unkind sentiments and abandon yourself to the visual pleasure she offered. It was Melania who chose this second route, maybe she was more inclined—naturally or for her own secret reasons—to deal with a swarm of emotions swiftly. She didn't even give me time to explain. As soon as she understood that my negative reply, whether true or false, would compel the girl to try on other articles of clothing, she got to her feet, and casually started up the game they had spent the whole morning playing. Gradually her friends followed suit. Instead of saying sorry, we have to leave now, as they had seemed so intent on doing, they started suggesting other outfits, some more enthusiastically than others, first feebly but soon with fervent participation. So, you don't like her in the cornflower blue? Well, how about this? Or this? Gradually, pleasure started to prevail over aversion. They went through the clothes they had tried on and discarded—how about this skirt? What do you think of these trousers? Lu, go try them on—turning even to Silvestro, as if they wanted to organize a performance for him, and reawaken his playful manner. As a result, and for the next good hour, Lu, poor girl, went in and out of the changing room in backless dresses, gowns with plunging necklines, maxi dresses, tea-length ones, short dresses, as well as skirts and shirts, blouses and sweaters, flared trousers and pegged ones, blazers and cardigans, bustiers, trench coats with hoods, raincoats, windbreakers with drawstrings, a collection of words that I had become perfectly at ease with: ruffled hem, boatneck, bell sleeves, cashmere details, feel how soft, how snug, how fluid, flowing, floaty, flu-flu-flu.

From my perspective, I was careful to say yes only to the items that Lu, whose face was no longer sallow, no long puffy with fatigue, seemed to enjoy wearing. I also pretended that the clothes moved entirely of their own accord, I avoided looking at the ladies and kept as far away as possible from Silvestro. He—and I feel I can say this with certainty—saw the girl not only when she came out dressed, but also in his imagination, in the changing room, out of breath, perspiring, taking off a blouse, letting a skirt drop to the floor, stepping into a pair of trousers, one leg first, then the next. Actually, I think he was ever more bothered by the growing suspicion that I, at eighty years old, still looked at things the way he did. But in this he was wrong, I didn't possess that gaze anymore, and besides, I had never been like him; I had torn that look out of my eyes immediately after my mother died. Now all I was trying to do was extract a living, quickened mother out of the body of Lu, a totally different woman from the one who had appeared earlier in the cream-colored foulard, on the cusp of a terrible death. I longed for my healthy mother, under the age of thirty, glowing and kind, capable of making people jealous and then taming that feeling with kindness and affection.

Outfit after outfit, this version of my mother gradually stepped out of Lu's body as she was looking in the mirror. While trying on a black dress, I saw her delicately smooth down the fabric over her hips. She smiled gently at herself, mouth slightly open, eyes communicating consent. She turned to the right, trying to see herself in profile, her hands gliding over her bottom to make sure the fabric fell well, pursing her lips and posing in ways that had absolutely nothing to do with her long, hard days. I watched her the way I did when I was ten years old, during her secret performances, when she became the woman my father saw as the definition of vanity—I've ineffectively written about this so many times—you're so vain, Rusinè, vain, vain, vain. I could never ignore how the sound of that adjective, with its offensive overtones, reached my ears, surrounded by thousands of other words in dialect, tucked deep inside my father's jealous voice, as he saw in that body of new clothes some kind of violation that needed to be punished, a form of disobedience, an indecent fantasy, artfully combined to create disorder, a form of escape, a possible farewell. Hiding in my corner, I tried—I still try, I'm trying even now—to grab hold of the moments before that word came unstitched and ruined, before my pleasure in admiring her admire herself was ruined. In those instants she was a phenomenal woman who had managed to flee from herself and her own life. I spied on her and thought: how pretty my mother is when she is vain, oh how splendidly and vainly you fortify your body, mamma; I was bewitched by her vanity, I pulled her away from my father who took her apart with his voice, I continue to pull her to safety even if she is only a shadow of a shadow of a shadow.

Bodies evaporate, can't do anything about it, ambitions are lost, possibilities dissipate. But that's not happening to Lu, at least not for now. She firmly shut the door on my dying mother and, dress after dress, one content expression after the next, she has regained her healthy color, she's strong again, she releases the light of someone who wants to leap to the top of the world, whatever the cost.

"What do you think of the trench coat?" Evelina asked me.

"I'm not sure, I'd like to see it again."

"Show him again, Lu, please. This time with the little beige sweater and brown trousers."

The girl obeyed and a few minutes later stepped out looking like a determined young woman on her way to an important meeting that she can't miss even though it's about to rain, I can almost hear the rumble of thunder in the distance. She glanced around and pulled up the well-cut hood, which framed her face so delicately that all the ladies present sighed with pleasure—oh how lovely, Lu—protecting herself from the rain and wind, from storms, from downpours, drizzle, from the end of it all.

"I'll take it," I said.

A startled Silvestro jumped to his feet. "Well done, your granddaughter will be pleased," he said snidely.

None of the ladies laughed or smiled. Chatting among

themselves, they walked over to the counter and picked up their shopping bags as Lu wrapped up my purchases, and I paid.

"Our job," Silvestro spoke up, trying to reacquire his playful tone, "is to pull out the wallet when needed."

His wife ignored him and looked at me. "Leave me your cell phone. I'll bring you everything myself."

Silvestro tried to wheedle his way in: I have to deliver the kayak to him anyway, I can do it. Evelina glanced at him sharply, and he looked down. While I wrote down my phone number, her voice rang out clearly. "I'll run over, it doesn't cost me a thing."

20.

I stopped in the piazza, at the café under the pergola, and watched the ladies walk to their cars. They seemed happy. I probably exaggerated their attachment to Silvestro. Who can really say what goes on in other people's minds: I am me, they are them, and who knows what kinds of pushing and shoving they've had—and will have—to deal with.

The light was gray, humid. At the end of the Corso, puffs of clouds hung over the low buildings like small explosions. Eventually Evelina and Silvestro came out and walked in the direction of the sea, she quickly, wrapped up in her thoughts, he lazily, looking at his cell phone.

I ordered a tuna sandwich and a beer. From where I was sitting, I'd be able to see when Lu closed the shop for lunch break, after tidying up. Maybe she'll hurry off to the beach, I thought, it's already two o'clock. But she didn't. She pulled down the security gate and then stood there for a moment, writing something on her phone. She seemed bothered; eventually she brought the phone up to her mouth and recorded a long voice message. Then she crossed the piazza and stopped at my table.

"Join me, please. Have something to eat," I asked invitingly.

"No, thank you, I have to run."

"To your canoe?"

"To my son."

I left the last few bites of my sandwich on my plate and stood up. "He's a nice kid, Niní."

"Thanks, but please don't say any more about the giant squid. That's all he ever talks about now."

"I thought his father told him stories about sea monsters."

"With his father it's a game, but he took your giant squid seriously, and now he has nightmares."

"I'm sorry, I made a mistake."

"What you did back there was a mistake, too."

"With the clothes?"

"Yes."

"Didn't you enjoy trying them on?"

She tipped her head to one side ambiguously: it could have been a yes or a no, or maybe just disappointment. "I already have a hard enough time making sense of things, and when you add whatever it is you're thinking, I go off the rails."

"I'll be more careful."

"I say it not just for me, but for you, too. People here might seem friendly and honest, but they're not. How much did he want for the kayak?"

"Eight hundred and fifty euro."

"He ripped you off."

"I know."

She peers at me carefully, as if seeing me for the first time. "Are you good with a paddle?"

"I've never even tried."

"Never? Not even when you were young?"

"No."

"Then why did you buy a kayak?"

"I saw you out canoeing and was hoping that you'd teach me."

"Are you joking? I don't have time."

"Oh well. If I'm no good, I'll only have wasted a little money."

"You sure like to throw it around."

"I don't spend a thing for months on end, and then I regret it. Why have money if you don't spend it?"

"Are the clothes you bought really for your mother?" she asked with delicate irony.

"Yes."

She turned to look at the row of small clouds resting on top of the purplish mountains, then turned and stared deep into my eyes. "What do you want from me?"

"I already told you: to learn how to kayak as well as you canoe."

Her eyes lit up with happiness. "My canoe is old. You have no idea what I could do with a kayak. I hope that cheater sold you a decent boat, at least."

"I hope so too."

"Silvestro has heaps of money and always wants more. That's just the way he is: he thinks he can buy anything with money."

"Does he manage?"

"Anyone can. All you have to do is make someone desire

something, then say: if you give me this, I'll give you what you want."

"Is he good?"

"At what?"

"At making people desire things?"

"Pretty good."

"I noticed he treats you with respect."

She repressed a laugh into a barely audible gasp. "That man has no idea what respect is." Then she looked around uneasily, checked her cell phone, and repeated that she had to run. "I'd like to check out the kayak, though, one of these days," she added casually.

"With pleasure. Say hi to Gino, he's a nice kid."

"Thanks, I will."

She walked swiftly across the scorching piazza, her sparkly sneakers glittering in the light.

21.

I've been sitting on the beach for a few hours now: reading, writing, erasing, watching the late afternoon waves. Edged with foam, they roll in slowly and break high, high up on the shore, reflecting the pale sky.

I brought my cell phone with me and I switch on the ringer, certain that Evelina will call.

The phone rings around five and she says she'll come by after closing up. We can have a bite to eat, I say wanly. She turns me down but is glad to have been asked: another time with pleasure, she says, but today she'll just drop off the packages and run.

I leave the beach reluctantly. Walking up the sandy slope

towards the steps is more tiresome than usual. I skirt pieces of driftwood, I'm careful of the rusty wire fence that pokes out of the sand here and there, I swear out loud when a thorn gets stuck in the heel of my right foot, the one with the blackened nail, which is growing looser every day.

I stop. Suddenly I feel like I can write with clarity about the gold-edged figurine that got away from me a few days ago. The words are so simple that I jot them down in pencil while standing on the empty beach, surrounded by bottle caps, bird feathers, purple warty crab shells.

The thing—I write—that for simplicity's sake I called a figurine came out of my own body, it slipped out from under my dying nail like an opportunistic rat leaping from a sinking ship.

That's it. I can't be any more precise than that for now. I put away my notebook and examine the thorn: it's dry, dark, and shaped like a small isosceles triangle. I pick up my chair and beach bag and limp home.

I take a quick look around and realize that I can't possibly welcome Evelina into such a mess. I try to clean up. I put Maurizio's contraption away with the vacuum, mops, brooms, pails, buckets, and detergents. I look for the four hundred euro I found on the beach—where are they? Oh yes, on the bedside table—and examine the money clip carefully. It is gold, not *like* gold or *as if* gold, and it has the weightiness of an object that has been carefully crafted. Looking at it carefully, I can make out a very stylized S, but it could also be an I or a P, or no letter at all, maybe it's a tree, a flute, or a snake. I leave the money on the bedside table, bring the money clip into the kitchen, and put it in the cupboard next to some stale bread, sugar, coffee, and a bottle of olive oil. I wait, dopey from the sound of the sea.

Evelina shows up at eight-thirty. She walks in exuberantly, hands me two large shopping bags filled with the clothes I bought, and then threatens me. If I find out—she says—that they're not for your granddaughter but for some Ukrainian floozy that has duped you, well, I'll be very disappointed, Nico, and I won't want to see or hear from you ever again. I reassure her—no floozies—and say, come in and sit down. At first she refuses but then accepts. I lead her out onto the terrace, what's left of the deep red sunset is now almost entirely swallowed up by the blue of night. I open a beer for her, offer her a few tarallini from Puglia, and I have a glass of milk.

"My dinner," I say.

"So that's how you stay so slender."

"I'm saggy, not slender."

"You're not saggy, my husband is saggy, and he's much younger than you."

"He doesn't seem saggy to me."

"He does to me, and I have the distinct misfortune of sitting across from him as he gobbles up breakfast in his underpants and t-shirt. You saw how unbearable he is, didn't you? This morning I wanted to disappear; I apologize."

"He seemed cordial and full of life."

But Evelina shakes her head, looking like someone who thinks: so you got tricked, too, and then she goes on to angrily describe just what a lowlife he is. With a barage of clichés, which I envy her given their clarity, she paints an image of Silvestro as a thief, opportunist, and whoremonger. With everything he has stolen and trafficked—he robbed me of my inheritance from my father—he managed to start a number of successful businesses: the sporting goods store, two very popular ice cream shops, a restaurant on the pier that's always crowded, and the boutique, my boutique—she emphasizes—which he calls his because he can't conceive of something being yours, he only knows how to say mine, mine, mine. And politics? Over the past ten years, he's held important positions in all the city councils, and yet never once got in trouble for problems he created for others. And women, well, holy Christ, the man could never contain himself, he's cheated on me with every whore in this dull town, both the ones that know they are and the ones that don't. .

I listen with composure and let her vent, I figure this is what she came here for. Now and then, I feebly try to downplay what she is saying, pointing out that while her husband may have many flaws, you have to admit that he also has a good nose for business, he's sharp, and he's terribly manly. She agrees straight away, actually she seems almost pleased to hear me say it, and she uses my observations to explain why she has put up with the man. But I just can't take it anymore—she starts to get angry again—he disgusts me, and she goes on to complain about all the wrongs she's been subjected to in the past and is still today.

"Well," I say at one point and without much conviction, "keep in mind how hard it is for anyone to find a balance between virtues and vices, and if he manages to do so, well then, hats off to him."

"Balance?" she bursts out. "You know what balance is for him? Balance for him means pretending not to be angry when he really is, pretending that he's not getting revenge when he really is. He's the kind of person who says he can't live without you—while he's killing you."

This time I say nothing. I watch her finish her beer and stare pensively at a faded sliver of red that separates the dark sea from the sky. Then, with a sigh, she starts to stand up and says: thank you for listening to me. She gets to her feet with some hesitation, we go inside, and she mumbles: well, I guess I'll be leaving now. I walk towards the door but she doesn't move.

"Nothing nice has happened to me for a long time now," she says.

"That's simply not true: you live in a city full of light, you have good taste, and you're good at your work. I also noticed how much you like your assistant and her son, there's nothing more pleasant than being surrounded by people that you like."

"Yes, but something else is missing."

"What?"

She comes up close, she's about ten centimeters shorter than me, she has a voluminous head of hair, plump shoulders and large, high breasts.

"I'd like to be kissed," she says, turning ashen with emotion.

I, too, become emotional. I feel the great effort that it took to say those words and I am moved.

"I'm old, Evelina," I say softly. "If I lift an arm, my knee hurts. If I roll over in bed, I get a cramp in my ankle. I use any energy I have left to keep aches and pains at bay."

"Just a kiss, that's all I'm asking for."

I take her face in my hands and gently graze her lips with my own, once, twice, and then stroke her neck as I pull away. She, however, wraps her arm around my neck in a movement that is both forceful and affectionate, and kisses me lightly, making tiny smacking sounds, then pushes her chest and belly up close and rams her tongue in my mouth.

We end up kissing for a long time, I discover in her

mouth the memory of other kisses. She stops for a second, just long enough to open her veiled eyes, close them again, and kiss me some more. Her tongue is smooth and her mouth is warm, we explore each other's oral cavities darting and colliding. I think of the way she said *just*, as in *just a kiss*, it seems so artificial. Once, Laura said the same thing to me, in tears: it was just a kiss. As if a kiss were nothing, which is ridiculous, what a senseless hierarchy we use to measure things. Since a kiss—we say to ourselves—takes place in the nobler parts of our body, we think of it as something sweet, respectable, and even if it might trigger a reaction in the genital area, there's nothing obscene about it. This is not the case if we use our tongue or any other body part in the lower regions of the body. Then it's not *just a kiss*, then there's something salacious about it, pleasure is involved, it's sex, and sex brings joy as well as great suffering; tragedy is always right around the corner. No—I remember shouting back at Laura with tears in my eyes—kissing that second-rate piano player on the mouth was a far greater act of intimacy than anything else. But here, now, with Evelina, I'm glad we're probing each other's mouths, exchanging saliva. I haven't kissed anyone like this in years.

"I really do need to go now," she says, untangling herself from the embrace, pulling her body slowly away from mine, wiping her moist lips with the back of her index finger. I open the door for her.

"Why did you buy a kayak?" she asks on the threshold.

"For fun."

"Stay away from my husband, he's a bad man."

I nod gently. "Will you tell him?" I ask.

"About what?"

"That we kissed."

A look of hopeless grief fills her eyes. "Probably."

22.

After I hear Evelina drive away, I unwrap the articles of clothing that Lu tried on and that I purchased: the hooded trench coat, a blouse, a sweater, a cardigan, a pair of trousers, a skirt. I look at them without any interest whatsoever. They're the remnants of the morning I spent in the shop and nothing more. As a young man it was deceptively easy to manipulate real facts, use them to churn out fictional stories with elements of truth, but as an old man my feeble efforts lead only to despair.

I turn off all the lights in the house except the one on the bedside table. I try to understand what has happened, what is happening. Rosa's ghost appeared in the shop, took part in the little fashion show, imbued herself into the shopgirl and all the other women present. Now she's here, she has arrived via the clothes that Lu tried on and which Evelina delivered to me with her kisses of unhappiness and suffering. My mother brought all of us along with her: us kids, still young, and my father, who is about thirty-five years old. He's not in a good mood, he never could stand men like the owner of the sporting goods store. Womanizers set his teeth on edge, especially if they're married or have girlfriends. Once I hinted at a dalliance I had with a married woman—I was a young man at the time—and he, who relished talking about sex in the most vulgar way possible any chance he got, glared at me with disapproval: taking another man's woman is low, kid, only cowards do that.

My mother, meanwhile, enjoys stories about women who overcome all odds in the name of love, especially those about oppressed women who courageously fight back, often with tragic consequences. One of her favorite lines, a line that captures just how empathetic she was—everyone liked Rosa, both men and women, precisely because of how easily she understood and accepted other people's weaknesses; my father meanwhile tried hard to be liked by telling funny stories but always ended up growing caustic and was consequently not well liked—one of her favorite lines, I was saying, was: he swore he loved her and so she. *Andsoshewhat?* my father would interrupt her to demand, and then he'd start screaming with rage: so if some bastard says to you, Rusinè, I love you, and then he swears it's true, you'll stop loving me and run off with him?

Their arguments often began with some kind of remark like that. A few words and soon enough they'd be taking turns wounding each other—he'd hurt her feelings and she'd hurt his—and it would quickly grow and multiply into shouting and crying, I can't take this anymore, I'm going to throw myself out the window. And all because my mother reacts to the way my father humiliates her, and because my father, once he flies off the handle, can't stand the fact that she reacts. Sleazy men who wheedle their way into families by pretending to be friends with the husband but who then actually try and screw the wives are his most detested enemies. And the women who listen to those pieces of shit, the women who fall prey to their flattery, and even fall in love with them are worse, Rusinè, worse than whores. The idea that his wife might belong to that category of women transforms him instantly from doting husband to ruthless assassin, to the extent that sometimes it feels like he doesn't love her if he's not torturing her.

Their shadows push and shove each other, they explode out of my head, and they chase each other through the scrub, crying out with both pleasure and pain. What a terrible thing it is to love and hurt someone at the same time.

Sometimes my mother hopes for a miracle and turns to Saint Cyrus, her favorite saint, to cure her husband of his jealousy. I believe that, for her, that saint—the only male figure he allowed her to spend time with—was vital not only because she hoped that he would keep us children healthy, but above all for how she hoped that he would make her husband normal. She considered my father extraordinary, and therefore crazy. On some days, happy ones, she found him more extraordinary than crazy, while on other deeply unhappy days he was more crazy than extraordinary. She didn't want him to be ordinary, just balanced, and for this she needed Saint Cyrus, whose life, death and miracles she knew inside out—and particularly his death.

Now I can't swear that all the images of the saint's martyrdom that continue to swirl through my mind were transmitted to me from her: she was an intelligent woman, and I rule out the possibility that her thoughts revolved solely around suffering and agony, although married life had dealt her more than her fair share. Even so—and putting aside for a moment the fact that all my religion teachers, with their so-called wholesome truths, instilled in me the belief that a love of God, torture, and blood co-exist on the same plane—I can still hear her husky, no-nonsense voice that I invented for her (how it really sounded, I just don't know) telling me what happened to Cyrus, the monk-doctor, and John, his soldier friend, when they arrived in the city of

Canopus, how they rushed to the local prison to assist four prisoners faithful to Christ: Athanasia and her three daughters, Theoctista, Theodota, and Theodossia, who were fifteen, thirteen, and eleven years old respectively.

Upon reaching the prison, the two men were promptly arrested under the order of prefect Siriano. Oh, what gory scenes ensued; from my earliest childhood memories I cull images of great atrocity. Cyrus and John were stripped naked in front of Athanasia, Theoctista, Theodota, and Theodossia, their cocks hanging like those of the horses that roamed the streets back then. The two men were flogged and beaten by angry soldiers with long sticks of gnarled wood as if they were unfeeling rocks and not men whose flesh bruised, tore, and bled down their backs, chests, backsides, and hairy thighs. Their arms and legs were pierced with long rusty nails, severing veins, arteries, nerves, bones. Their assassins held flaming torches up to their bodies, roasting them from head to foot, and especially around their open wounds. Vinegar and salt were then applied to the bleeding flesh with careful delight. And after all that, the two future saints, the doctor and the soldier, were forced to stand in cauldrons of boiling tar.

But then something happened in the story that I liked: the more atrocities that were inflicted on them by their wicked torturers, the more the doctor and soldier *rejoiced*, laughing at the cruelty to which they were subjected with peace in their hearts and cheer on their faces, as if they were at a sumptuous banquet and not being tormented.

I perceive something of my mother's ghost in the way the two men rejoiced at being martyred. In some dark corner of my childhood imagination, I grant her one of the splendid golden aureoles that Athanasia, Theoctista, Theodota, and Theodossia wore like much-coveted hats. Rosa was so devoted to the saint that I took my first communion, a day of great celebration, dressed in a monk's tunic and carrying a white candle; while my head was filled with wholesome truths, my eyes saw the horrors of their joyful martyrdom as if I had been there in person. There's a photo of me in my outfit standing next to her, and she looks beautiful, wearing an elegant dress she made especially for the occasion and a hat with a short dark veil; she's smiling, her expression shows pleasure. My father is in the picture, too, he's got his arm around her shoulder, it's clear they love each other. I visualize them and experiment with dressing her in all the clothes I bought this morning, from the blouse to the trench coat. I pull the hood up over her pitch black hair, it looks good, she seems happy. But it doesn't last; the present day and Lu muscle their way in. The girl chases my mother back into dark despair, she has her own ideas and wants to pursue them. For as long as I've lived, I've always believed that it's impossible to fully experience joy without also knowing boiling hot tar.

23.

I didn't say a single word to anyone for a few days, but I wrote and erased many. In the meantime, the sea grew so warm and still that it almost stopped moving. It doesn't make loud noises at night anymore, it just gasps.

I used the metal detector a couple of times but all I found was a small medallion that showed some kind of Jesus figure sitting on a throne. I even took a few dips to cool off, as the air felt heavier than usual. I made my way into the water, cloudy with seaweed, with the usual caution; old people fear hurting themselves as much as cowardly children do, only they don't have strong young parents to hold onto for protection. Initially the cool water felt soothing, but soon enough, following a tried and true storyline, I felt cold. So I'd put on my robe and rub my hair dry but then, soon enough, I'd feel hot again. These fluctuations in temperature were so frustrating, I got angry with my old age, with these aches and pains, the instability, the sore throats, clogged ears, the fear of dying and that of living too long, the thought of how wonderful it is to see your children grow into adults but not to see them shrivel up, no, no, no, mother of mercy, I was all sweaty again.

I was about to take off my robe—it was four o'clock in the afternoon, the sun was still strong—when suddenly little Niní appeared by my side in his bathing suit. He looked no different from my own grandchildren when—as little kids—they'd suddenly appear on the beach—ciao, nonno—and then run off and play. I took notice of them distractedly, ciao, I'd say, and they'd blend into the book I was reading. They were there and not there. Ghosts of the future, they stood like young leaves on an olive tree in August, barely visible next to the older yellow-spotted leaves with "occhio di pavone."

The little boy looked up at me. "From far away, I thought you were a monk."

"It's a costume. Now I'll show you who I really am." I threw my robe onto the chair and stood in front of him in my ridiculous faded blue swim trunks. "Here I am."

"You're older than you look."

"It depends on the day. Today is a bad day: I'm as old as I'll ever be. I feel weak. And look at this, not a single muscle. I can't even keep my eyelids open."

"How will you go out in the kayak?"

"How do you know about the kayak?"

"My father's bringing it to you now," the boy said, pointing towards a hollow in the green scrub held up by a dark cluster of branches. Walking slowly, the heavy Maurizio made his way out of a sort of tunnel in the undergrowth, carrying a gray-blue kayak on his back.

"Let's go help him," I said.

"He doesn't want help."

"Let's go anyway."

Sweating and panting heavily, Maurizio was also carrying the paddle and pump. I made him put the craft down and together we carried it to the shore: I held the bow, he the stern and the pump, while Niní had the paddle. As soon as we set it down, the child leapt into it.

"Get out of there, or you'll get it all sandy," Maurizio ordered.

"Let him play," I said.

"He'll ruin it."

"No, he won't."

Maurizio didn't give up. "Get out of there. It's his boat and he should be the first one to use it."

"But he said he feels weak."

"It's true," I said. "If I ran into the giant squid today I wouldn't have the strength to chase it or flee from it."

Niní looked at me, puzzled. "My mother said that giant squids don't exist. And my father says they only exist in imagination."

"I'm not your father," Maurizio corrected him.

Niní grinned tolerantly. "He's joking. He always says that. Can you push me into the water?"

Maurizio didn't mind, so I pushed the kayak into the water.

"Do you know how to paddle?" I asked the boy.

"I'm super good at it."

"Like your mother?"

"Even better."

Maurizio spoke up but in a gentle way. "You're not super good at it, big guy. No going farther out than two meters. And if you disobey, I'll come over and show you what's what."

The boy picked up the paddle and looked at me carefully. "Have you ever even seen a giant squid?"

"Not personally. But a friend of mine saw one chasing a swimmer a long time ago."

"Here?"

"No, in a place called Serk."

"Is that near here?"

"No, it's very far away. Anyway, they killed it."

"How?"

"I don't know. But someone else I know, a man named Gilliatt, killed an even bigger one. He cut off its head with a knife the way a dentist pulls a tooth."

"I don't have a knife."

"That's alright. You have to stay near the shore, and anyway, I'd hand you one."

I watched Niní: he diligently stayed nearby and handled the paddle, which was much longer than he was tall, with competence; he cut cleanly through in the water in the direction of the pier, then turned around and came back. He really was good, I said to Maurizio.

"It's all thanks to his mother," he replied with a frown. "She wants the kid to know how to do everything well, to stay grounded even when he's out on the water."

"She likes people who are concrete?"

"What do I know, that's her business. But she definitely wants to raise her son to be practical, and not to live in a fantasy world, that's why she got so angry about your giant squid story."

"Practicality without imagination is flawed. Stories are good and useful precisely because they train the brain not to be satisfied with appearances, and to look beyond."

Maurizio's face clouded over. "Sometimes behind appearances there's just stupidity. People try to pass themselves off as special, and often we believe them, but really they're just stupid, and they always will be."

I sat down on the sand with a heavy groan and invited him to join me. I felt the need to talk to someone and was glad that Maurizio had delivered the kayak and not Silvestro. Despite his girth, he sat down with great agility.

"Stupidities like this?" I asked, showing him the medallion I found with the metal detector.

He examined it carefully. "Exactly. Not worth a thing."

"That's not true for a believer. If a person with faith wears this medallion around their neck or wrist, they don't need to search for the meaning of life or why certain things happen to them. They have it."

I went on to tell him how, as a boy, I wanted to be a monk so that I could spend my entire life sitting in a cell and studying, then go on to become a great writer of works full of wholesome truths.

"But, my dear friend, it didn't last," I confessed. "The flesh is weak, or rather, strong. I became a mediocre hack and atheist, and disgusted by how badly the world functioned, I wanted to contribute to subverting it, rebuilding it, making it perfect. But that didn't work out either. Time passed, the world became even more imperfect, and all I had left was my obsession with telling stories about minor events of everyday life."

"And here I was thinking you were a retired judge who performed comedy on TV in his spare time," Maurizio said with hesitant irony. "Instead I learn that first you were a monk, then you became a subversive, and now you're a writer?"

"When you fail at everything, you try anything."

"Are you working on a book now?"

"Yes."

"Here, at the beach?"

"Yes."

"What's it about?"

"It's a summary of everything I haven't been able to write well."

"What does writing well even mean?"

"Finding the right words that give meaning to all the pointless things that happen to us while we're alive."

"Are you famous?"

"Hardly."

"How about as a judge? Or comic? Or monk?"

"No."

"But you've managed to save up some money."

"Yes, this I have done."

He couldn't help but laugh loudly, mouth open wide; I noticed he was missing an incisor.

"So why do you still care about words and meaning? You did good, that should be enough," he said.

I didn't mention how—despite the fact that old age was increasingly a balcony from which one had a view on meaninglessness—I didn't want to give up, that I was scared of falling. Instead I nodded at Niní passing by in the kayak and said, "My mind has gotten used to it, I can't do anything about it, it has its needs. Right now, for example, that boy is merely an effect of the light. And yet I can't deny that if I place him in a story and weave it together with the little bit that I know about you, his mother, and Evelina, together with a little bit of my imagination of him out hunting for a giant squid—detailing it with language, in other words—that I might actually make something, that I might find the thread, however tangled."

Maurizio must not have liked my comparison because he looked annoyed.

"So, essentially, you like wasting time."

"Why do you say that?"

He ran his hand through his hair and then smoothed it down again. "People do horrible things to strip meaning from others, only to then impose their own on them."

"I don't understand."

"There's nothing to understand. Things don't have meaning now and they never did. Not for us mammals, not for reptiles, not for half-reptile half-mammals, not even for that kid. There's no meaning in science and definitely no meaning in religion. The only god I like is the one who eliminates his creations at regular intervals when he realizes they have neither head nor tail. You can forget medallions, forget threads."

I looked at him keenly. He had grown passionate and his passion had led him to speak words of deep affliction more eloquently than those uttered by Ivan Karamazov.

"A thread always has its reality," I put forth.

"In words. But when you crash into it without artifice, you get decimated."

"Is that what happened to you?"

"Yes."

"Did you get hurt?"

"Yes."

"When?"

He reacted as if my request for chronological context was an insult and started digging angrily in the sand.

"I'm sorry, I can't tell you that," he almost-whispered. "It's my business and I want to keep it that way. I don't want someone to give it some kind of meaning, the next thing you know, it gets fried up all golden and served like an artichoke."

I nodded—forgive me, I said—even though it sounded like it had been a turning point for him. But it was clear that he wasn't going to tell me, that telling constituted some kind of violation, or maybe even an affectation.

"Is that what you taught at school—that life has no meaning?" I asked.

He was puzzled for a few seconds. School? He looked at me wide-eyed.

"I taught much worse," he said with a burst of cheer. "I taught history, geography, when people were born, when they died, all sorts of terrible things. Then I'd say to my students: standing before you is someone who, in order to stay calm, glosses over other people's words. I produce practically no original thoughts. Actually I'm terrified to even really think. And if a person can't handle thinking seriously, how can he possibly teach you the only thing that matters—how to have the will to understand until you die of fear?"

I felt like laughing. "Is that why they fired you?"

"Hardly. I told you, I'm naturally odious."

"Odious to everyone?"

"Yes."

"Even to your wife?"

"Ex-wife. Of course, even her. Ever since school."

"Was she a good student?"

"Excellent. But Lu is an indefinite creature: one day she's standing with her feet firmly planted on the ground, the next day her head is in the clouds. There's no ruling out that she actually loves giant squids more than we, the people who invent them, do."

Then he suddenly started yelling at Niní who was paddling by for the umpteenth time.

"That's enough, you troublemaker. The gentleman wants his kayak back right now."

Niní looked at me beseechingly. "Do you really need it?"

"Yes, he does," Maurizio replied for me.

"Please, papà, just a little longer."

"I'm not your father, and get out of that thing immediately, or I'll come out there and smack you out of it."

The child looked at him and said, you're stupid and you say stupid things. Then he slowly turned the kayak around with an extra wide maneuver and made his way towards the shore with a frown on his face.

Maurizio leapt to his feet with agility.

"The kid is right. Everything I say is stupid," he said uneasily.

"No, not at all. It feels good to talk to a friend."

I tried to get to my feet but had a hard time; he took my arm and helped me up.

"I hate to do this, but I need to ask you for something," he then said.

"What?"

"My metal detector. I'll lend it to you again, but I have an urgent job to do now."

I liked the way he used the word job. Although he said it with a hint of irony, it showed me that he did not consider walking up and down the beach waiting for it to beep a hobby.

"Did someone lose something?" I asked.

"A pin."

I pointed at the boat that Niní was struggling to drag ashore.

"Is the person who hired you the same one who asked you to bring me the kayak?"

He shook his head. "Unfortunately not, Silvestro is generous and I would've earned well. I'm doing it as a favor for that troublemaker's mother, and so, for free."

24.

Maurizio and I carried the kayak back to the wooden steps, Niní followed unhappily with the paddle and pump. The child wanted us to leave it near my building, in the garden, so it would be safe. I decided to leave it next to Lu's red canoe.

"Someone's going to steal it," the boy said.

"Now who would do something like that?"

He squinted. "Me."

"But you already have a canoe."

"It's not mine, it's my mother's, and it's old and ugly."

"Here's what we'll do: I'll leave a note in my will that says when I die, you will inherit my kayak."

"When are you going to die?"

Maurizio swatted the back of his head. "Don't be rude."

I came to Niní's defense. Fair question, I said. And then I answered by saying that I didn't know for sure but definitely soon: my body ached, I often felt dizzy, I frequently lost my balance, and the things I cared for most were quickly disappearing.

"You're in amazing shape," Maurizio said, hoping to cheer me up. "Evelina even said you're handsome."

"Evelina would say anything just to get on her husband's nerves."

He waggled his large head from side to side, maybe, maybe not, and followed me inside; Niní chose to stay behind to guard the kayak.

"Something smells familiar," Maurizio said, following me to the metal detector.

"Basil, maybe, I have a pot of it on the windowsill that I enjoy using."

"No, not basil."

"Then it's the scent of money," I said with a laugh and told him how, thanks to his device, I not only found the medallion with Jesus on it but four hundred euro, too.

"With the medallion?"

"Yes, buried in the sand. I'll show you." I went to my room to get the money. "It looks like the medallion was worth something after all," I said when I got back.

He was amazed. "You found it right next to the money?" he mumbled.

"Yes."

"I've never been that lucky. You found money not once, but twice."

"See? It's a sign. It means I'm your lucky charm. And

seeing how the contraption is yours, so is the money. I want you to take it."

"No. That's kind of you, but no."

"I insist. All I need is the medallion, it's a game for me, I stick one thing to another and see where it leads. But for you, it's work. Take the money, what do I need it for? There's nothing crazier than money."

Unlike with the fifty euro the time before, Maurizio gave in and accepted almost immediately, but on one condition. "Only if you agree to 'rent' the metal detector from me for the month and have this be the price."

I nodded and tucked the cash into the breast pocket of his sweaty shirt. "But you have to take the metal detector until you find your ex-wife's pin."

"Thank you."

"No. Thank *you*."

He picked up the contraption and started to walk towards the door, then hesitated.

"That smell, it's so strange . . . "

While he walked back down the wooden steps to Niní, I quickly gathered up all the clothes I had bought, tossed them into the two shopping bags that Evelina had used to deliver them, and caught up with father and son, who were arguing near the kayak. Niní was sitting in it and pretending to paddle. Maurizio was gesturing for him to get out.

"You might as well go home," I said to the boy. "The giant squid got away—for today anyway."

He grinned complicitly. "Did you see it?"

"Yes, it swam off, impossible to catch it now. But you can always come back, the kayak will be here waiting for you. But first, I have a favor to ask: give this stuff to your mother, tell her she can do whatever she wants with it."

Maurizio cast a puzzled glance at me. The child's expression changed, suddenly he looked like someone with an important mission. Fine, he said, and he was about to take the bags when he glanced inside and then looked up at me with hesitation.

"These clothes smell like my mother," he said.

I gave the boy and his father a friendly half-smile.

"No," I said. "That's my mother's smell, they're hers."

25.

Niní and Maurizio walked off quarreling. I sat on the terrace for a while watching the calm sea, then went back down to the beach and, with great effort, dragged the kayak to the water's edge. I set it afloat and, after several awkward attempts, managed to climb in.

Straight away I felt very unsteady, the boat seemed to constantly be on the verge of capsizing. And I wasn't quite sure how I should sit, where to put my feet and legs. Nevertheless, I used the paddle to push myself out into open water, only two or three meters away from the shore, not much farther than Niní had gone. My goal was to head towards the pier while staying parallel to the dove-gray shoreline, but I quickly realized that I didn't know how. I struggled to move forward in a straight line. Without intending to, I kept heading right, towards the horizon; each time I realized it, I got scared and tried to recoup by paddling to the left, back towards the shore. But even in this, I tried too hard and kept almost running aground, which meant that I had to then paddle forcefully to the right again. So I zig-zagged for a while until I started to get the hang of it, and then went up and down the coast until sunset, fifty meters towards the pier, a sloppy u-turn, then fifty meters back.

Now and then I noticed people walking on the beach, not many couples, mainly solitary figures out for a stroll. They looked at me distractedly and kept walking. At one point I thought I recognized Melania, her bright white hair up in a pony tail, she was jogging, wearing a two-piece exercise outfit that dug deep into her slender body. I saw her wave but I didn't dare reply as I was afraid of dropping the paddle. She continued on towards the pier, glancing back now and then to make sure she hadn't made a mistake.

It wouldn't have been her fault, maybe I actually was a mistake. I might have looked like an eighty-two year old man with four children and six grandchildren sitting in an inflatable gray-blue kayak, but in reality, the I who was paddling in opaque waters a few meters from the shore was still a child who had been protecting himself for decades by lying to and about himself, mixing and muddling his being out of figures and figurines composed of words without any grand ambition.

It's anxiety-inducing to have grand ambitions. As I paddled along, I recalled the pages and pages of pretentious writing I composed as a young man. Back then my goal was to write at least one masterpiece, the kind of book that lasts for centuries and includes scores of events, much philosophy and ethos, a model for future generations. I tended to construct tumultuous and deep characters whom I attributed with passion, imagination, and intelligence, unhappily wallowing in the mysteries of both animate and inanimate matter. But, shortly after turning twenty, I realized just how inept I was and, in order to fight my dismay,

I carved out a small niche for myself and my mediocrity. I remember thinking: if I don't have the stuff to produce great works, I'll focus on producing minor ones, I'll make do with the odds and ends I have. And so, deep inside my cave, all hunched over, my shoulders curving like a billhook, I started to assemble—without ever going overboard, without ever pretending that I knew things I did not—simple men and women who knew nothing of physics or astrophysics, algebra or chemistry, who had no scientific understanding of their own souls or those of others, who couldn't see far into the future or look deep into themselves, people who didn't experience things passionately.

I don't know what compelled me to spend most of my time like that, refraining from aiming high but not entirely giving up either. Maybe I've always been scared of my own heartbeat, scared it would beat so fast that I'd come undone and fall to pieces, so I intentionally lowered my temperature, chilled my blood and words. Come to think of it, as far back as I can recall, I never imagined myself a living and breathing creature of flesh and blood, but an animate puppet, a puppet who existed among girl puppets and boy puppets, and this mise-en-scène calmed me. I worked on myself as if I were a device, regulating my volume, speed, and not just while writing, but whenever I encountered strong emotions in everyday life. Each time I fell in love, for instance, I deliberately lowered the temperature of my fervor and passion and artfully made myself lukewarm. These needs—I would tell myself—appear with urgency, become pressing and insistent, and ultimately deflate me. The body is a spring mechanism; if I don't get wound up, I can get by without anything, or anyone. Sure, when a woman said yes it was exciting, I was happy when I gained their consent.

But then a part of me would almost immediately grow suspicious of the excess and push away loud or sappy expressions of love, and occasionally this made me bitter: why do you have to be like this, I'd ask myself, you're so stupid, just relax, let go, what's wrong with you.

I tried but I didn't succeed. Things were always great at the outset, I would sleep well and it felt wonderful to wake up next to a person you loved, to be able to reach out and touch their fingers, a foot, a hip, their breasts, their ass, or the exultant secrets of their genitals. Love truly has certain childish aspects to it; it's pure joy, an explosion of nicknames, phrases that are gloriously free of meaning—nonsense, essentially. Losing even a moment of the time spent falling asleep and waking up together hurt. Soon enough, though, I'd find myself craving distance, I'd grow anxious and start to sleep poorly. Happiness, when prolonged, felt like a waste. I'd get up, read, write. Soon enough, she—the women I loved, my Nina, Laura, Nora, with their different names but similar schemata—started to seem eager for something else, and started to pay more attention to her own things. The world was a woven wicker basket, and our love stories appeared to be made of the same material. We had so very many things to do, in addition to being happy. The past sixty years have been spent running from one conversation to the next, from deadline to deadline, pursuing interests, hobbies, books, money. I would come home—to any of the modest or elegant places I have lived—tired and absentminded and would run out in the morning tired and absentminded. I experienced pleasure with distraction, as I did happiness. Following the many joyful affirmations of my first true love and the many affectionate affirmations of my children's infancy, came one very long and angry no, which eventually turned icy cold and led to many small sad separations. Nina was heartbroken and resigned to single-handedly raising the children we had casually had together. Laura did the same but with bitterness for me and for all irresponsible, negligent men. Only Nora remained until the threshold of old age, gradually transforming love into indifference, expecting me to pretend that her emotional life, which unfolded entirely outside our relationship, didn't exist. Even my children, with whom I was close until they were about ten years old, left me, and having to choose they always chose their mothers, even though they were more distracted and weary than I was.

Ask all your girlfriends—Nora said before definitively moving into our only son's house—ask, and they'll tell you that you promise a great deal but never carry through. In fact, life with me was always never enough, of inferior quality. And whenever I fully realized that, I felt sad, and yet content for choosing to be mediocre. I didn't have some great stature to defend, I didn't have to hide my petty thoughts, such as the suspicion that the women I was involved with looked elsewhere for what I couldn't give them. The world was full of temptations, it was sneaky, convincing, a sticky mess, I knew it well. I was surrounded by a horde of married women who took on lovers as if they were honorifics. Why should the people I loved turn down countless attractive human beings, gentlemen who held some semblance of power, who used their bodies to guarantee their superiority?

How opaque sentimental life is, so full of hiding places. I never trusted anyone, not even Rosa—my father didn't trust her and he taught me, through his actions, not to trust her—and actually, she was the person I trusted least;

from a very young age she made me feel at risk of humiliation and abandonment. Just at risk, only a possibility, never an actual fact. None of my them—not Nora, Laura, or Nina—ever actually confessed the betrayals they engaged in probably to make up for my shortcomings. But I was so certain of it in my imagination that a significant portion of my affective life was spent pretending not to be the jealous man I was, and then breaking down periodically with total self-contempt. Tell me what happened. Nothing. I saw you, with my own two eyes. You're sick, you need help, you're seeing things that aren't there, as usual. I couldn't tolerate the thought that their joyful cries of yes, yes, yes that were so much a part of our early days—how beautiful those moments were, I remembered them well, I was nostalgic for them—were now being whispered to others to compensate for the angry utterances of no, no, no that stemmed from the distracted, arid love that I withheld from them. I heard the gentle lapping of long, deep kisses, the likes of which I hadn't given in ages. In my fantasies I could see Nora's elegant panties, Laura's bras, and Nina's underthings draped over chairs and on beds in rooms belonging to people I didn't know, or even ones I did, where they went in secret, their hearts beating rapidly with the novelty, whispering *it's me* into the building intercom. Girl puppets and boy puppets, I'd say to myself, always the same idiocies: love, sex, do you love me, I love you, that's all you think of, only the need for excitement and languor. Nonetheless, I understood why—I always understand why other people do things—and it hurt, so I would slip away like a water snake.

26.

My old and wandering mind ended up ruining my first attempt at navigation. I made a mistake with the paddle and hit the brim of my hat, causing it to fall in the water. Instinctively, I reached to the left to get it but leaned so far that the boat almost tipped over. Finally, I managed to scoop up the hat with one end of the paddle. I put it on my head even though it was dripping wet, and enjoyed feeling the seawater stream down my forehead and onto my shoulders. For a moment I didn't move: I was a scarecrow in a kayak, a scaregull, a scarewhale for when they breach with no warning.

Then Melania walked by again. When she saw me only a couple of meters out from shore, my hat soaking wet, the boat rocking slowly, me gripping the paddle tightly but with my hands on my thighs, she stopped.

"So, it really is you?"

"Who knows," I replied cheerfully.

"What are you up to?"

"I'm reviewing some of the key moments in my life."

"While sitting in a canoe? And not even paddling?"

"It's a kayak. It's comfortable but I'm not very good at it."

"I'm guessing Silvestro foisted it on you?"

"Yes."

"That man is capable of selling you his own mother."

"He has a mother?"

"She died two years ago, but if he needed to, he could peddle you a story that she's alive. He's a genius when it comes to business, he really knows how to make money."

"Luckily I don't need to buy a mother. I already have one, and she's a hundred and three."

"Wow, a hundred and three!"

"Yes."

"And in great health, I bet."

"Excellent."

"It must run in the family; clearly you inherited her longevity gene."

"Let's hope so."

"What did you get from your father?"

"Jealousy."

"Oh, that's too bad."

"Why?"

"Because jealousy is awful."

"It depends. If well-managed, it can be an exercise in deflection."

"Deflection of what?"

"The dramas of infidelity."

"That's funny. Tell Evelina that. It'll boost her spirits."

"Why, is Silvestro unfaithful to her?"

"You tell me what time it is, and I'll tell you who's he's fucking."

"Irmtraud?"

"Close, bravo, but wrong time of day."

We continued chatting for a bit: she stood on the shore, visibly jealous, I sat in the kayak, about a meter away from the water's edge, a little queasy from all the rolling and heat. Before leaving, she asked me one more question.

"So, what's your name?"

"Nicola Gamurra."

"Judge."

"Judge of the open seas."

"When are you returning to Rome, Nicola?"

"I plan on dying here."

"Good, then we'll have ample opportunity to enjoy other delightful conversations. You have the shrewdness of a refined gossip."

"Really?"

"Yes, and I'm not usually wrong about things like that."

"Can I gossip about you?"

"Go right ahead."

"What's your time slot?"

"You tell me. Let's see if you can guess."

"You don't have one anymore, you've given up your shift."

An expression of both annoyance and hurt crossed her pretty young face. "Like I said, a superb gossip. The only thing is you don't see the big picture."

"I've never been good at seeing the big picture."

"No one is, it's always changing. For now, that small and presumptuous man thinks he can have fun at our expense, but he's really just a poor devil, an idiot, because it's us girls who are screwing him. Goodbye Nicola, take care of yourself. And enjoy playing out your *Old Man and the Sea* fantasy; make Hemingway roll over in his grave."

"Am I convincing in the role of bold, jocular male, even in my old age?"

"Sure, we've all got to have fun somehow."

And off she ran towards an indiscriminate mashup of yellow, blue and a great deal of red that was the setting sun. I dragged the kayak up the beach and back under the steps, leaving a deep dark cleft in the sand behind me. The light of day grew evenly lilac; I realized that I was exhausted. I cut up some mozzarella and tomatoes, and dined with the mosquitoes. Now, in bed, in the dark, I see an infinite number of faces: each one stays only a couple of seconds before another one comes to take its place.

It's been happening a lot recently and each time it does I marvel at my ability to invent so many unknown faces. It's these images, much more than dark thoughts, that keep me up at night. Clear and assertive men and women. No bodies, just faces. They appear at the ends of streets I'm walking along or in movie theaters, or I see them in the church with yellow walls where I received my first communion dressed as a monk, or in the bedroom where I first took my time making love to a woman. And then, suddenly, each face grows distorted, they become cruel and painful scribbles, grave errors. Oh, how many mistakes I've made over the years: theoretical, ethical, grammatical, syntactical, sexual (I'm excessively polite), spelling. Have I always underestimated my own strengths? Has fear made my actions weak?

Perhaps, but it's too late now to remedy the situation, everything is falling apart: my body, the world, heaven, earth. Only the exercise of writing remains, it's a habit, I write even when I'm half-asleep. I do it mentally: arguments, separations, explosions and not just of families, children who pretend nothing is wrong but who break down in secret. Eventually I find the door that leads to sleep, and it has no threshold. For a few moments I enjoy the silence inherent in a hardback dictionary, now obsolete, sitting on a shelf. Nouns and adjectives all at rest, even verbs.

27.

The following day, in the afternoon, Maurizio showed up on the beach with his metal detector. A blackish silhouette, he moved slowly inland from the pier towards the distant mountains, which rested on vaporous pastel-colored clouds. With every beep—a crystal clear sound that pierced the silence of the beach and the lazily sloshing waves like a nail—he stopped, dug around in the sand, and then continued with his search.

I watched him from the terrace while enjoying my coffee, and when he reached the area below my house, I waved hello. He didn't wave back. Maybe he was too absorbed with his work.

So I shouted down to him. "Did you find the pin?"

"No, otherwise I wouldn't be here."

"Do you want a coffee?"

"No."

He must've been in a bad mood. He went up and down the beach, from the waterline to the scrub and back. Then Lu appeared, but with the kid, not alone. When Maurizio saw them, without interrupting his exploration of the beach with his machine, he made his way over to them. Maybe Lu had brought him Niní, or perhaps it was a casual encounter, hard to know. What happened after, though, was perfectly clear. As soon as Maurizio approached Lu, the metal detector started to beep faster and faster, beep-beep-beep, and it wouldn't stop.

The sound grew so strong that the child covered his ears with his hands, Lu shouted sourly at Maurizio, stop that thing right now, I have to make a phone call, and Maurizio stood there as if paralyzed. Then he switched off the device, the beeping stopped, and the entire landscape suddenly grew strangely quiet. Maurizio and Niní dropped to their hands and knees in great excitement. I watched the two figures dig, one burly, the other tiny, both in a frenzy, while Lu walked towards the water, talking on her phone.

The man and child burrowed eagerly for a while, and then with growing dismay. Maurizio called out to his ex-wife—nothing here, I'm turning it back on—maybe to warn her that he'd be making noise again. When he switched it on, the metal detector remained silent; even when he held it directly over the area that had once seemed so promising, the machine gave no sign of life. Lu, meanwhile, finished her call and went back to her son, who was still scrabbling in the sand. But as soon as she approached, the machine started beeping again.

I set down my empty coffee cup on the table and leaned out over the railing. At Maurizio and Niní's insistence, Lu took off her rings, earrings, and dress, but it was none of those—beep beep beep—it was her body.

How beautiful fairy tales are, I thought to myself. Down on the beach they began to celebrate, to the rhythm of the beeping. Maurizio exclaimed and laughed: Niní, your mother is a treasure, let's sell her, that's at least fifty kilos of gold. Lu laughed and shouted back: don't be ridiculous, throw that thing away, it's gone crazy, it's doesn't work. The child ran around hollering: we're rich, we're rich, my mother is a treasure.

After a while, Maurizio gave up and turned off the metal detector, the beeping stopped, and the party ended. The three of them, with the child in the middle, walked off towards the dark mouth in the green scrub.

I sat down on a deck chair and wrote in my notebook: my mother is a treasure. And then I read for a while.

28.

A day passed, then two, I grew lazy. There was hardly anything left in the fridge, but I wasn't hungry and managed just fine. I was out of bottled water, too, and the person who had rented me the house advised against drinking the tap water; I drank it anyway, it's slightly salty and not at all thirst-quenching. Neither Maurizio nor the kid came by, and that was a little disappointing. As for Lu, I figured that Gino was in town and that she was probably spending the little free time she had with him. I had no doubt in my mind, though, that soon enough she would reappear: tomorrow, the day after tomorrow, what did it matter, they're just words, they can be erased.

She came by today, alone, at half past one. I was sitting on my folding chair by the water's edge and heard the scuff of her shoes on the wooden steps, so I turned around. She had on the green dress with yellow flowers again, and she skipped quickly down the steps two at a time, a backpack on her shoulders. I waved to her, she didn't reply. Once she got to the beach, she ignored her red canoe and looked keenly at the kayak, then dragged it over to my chair.

"Is it worth the money I spent?" I asked her.

"It's good quality for its kind."

"So will you teach me how to use it?"

"I'm not sure. First you have to tell me what's really going on in that head of yours."

"There's nothing going on in my head."

"What about this dress, the trousers, the shirt, sweater, and trench coat?"

"They're gifts."

"You give too many gifts. You know I can't wear them here in town."

"You'll wear them this fall when you go away with your boyfriend."

"Why are you so generous?"

"Because you're helping me evoke my mother."

"The one who's a hundred and three years old?"

"Yes. That's how old she would've been if she hadn't died sixty years ago."

Lu was silent for a moment. "Did she look like me?"

"No, not in the slightest."

"So why . . . ?"

"Do I look like the kind of person who would buy a kayak?"

"Not at all."

"And yet I bought it, and right now I'm trying, with all the energy I have left, to paddle as well as you do."

"I don't understand you."

"I never really understood myself either; I've been lying and inventing my whole life, pretending that I do. And now that it's almost over, now that I'm old, I do whatever I want. But of course, if the clothes offend you, if you don't want to teach me how to handle this thing at least as well as your son does, then please just tell me—and I won't bother you anymore."

"Are you sure your motives aren't sexual?"

"Not that I am aware of. And, seeing how I don't really believe in psychoanalysis, the only things that really worry me are those I intentionally hide from myself. That said, I won't deny that you're very pretty and that seeing you in the trench coat with the hood up was particularly gratifying. But sexual motives, no, I assure you I have none."

"Promise that you won't start bothering me afterwards, promise that at a certain point you won't start saying things like 'I gave you this or that, now pay up.'"

"I promise."

"Good. One more promise."

"I'm listening."

"You told my son that he can use the kayak whenever he wants."

"That's true."

"You also convinced him that he can hunt for sea monsters with the kayak."

"No, not exactly. Just the giant squid."

"Exactly. Well I don't want you putting stupid ideas in his head. His father already babies him too much."

"I didn't invent the giant squid; Victor Hugo did."

"That doesn't change things. I don't want him growing up into a person who doesn't know what a Schuko adapter is."

"What's a Schuko adapter?"

"Be serious."

"I am, I really don't know what one is."

"I believe you. Do you promise me or not?"

"I promise that when I'm bored of the kayak I'll give it to Niní forever, under the condition that he uses it only when you're around and that he always asks your permission first."

"Why?"

"Because for me, *kayak* is just a mysterious word, while for the boy, thanks to you, it's something beautiful."

Suspicion returned to Lu's face. "You really do have money to throw away, don't you?"

"Lots."

"And what about the squid?"

"You'll have to take that up with Hugo, not with me."

"Don't be clever."

"I'm not. All I'm saying is that it's good to imagine terrible things that can never actually come to pass. That way, when bad things do happen, we're less frightened, and it's easier to find consolation."

She thought about this for a moment, staring at me with her mouth a little bit open. "Fine," she eventually said. "I'm not entirely convinced, but let's move on to lesson one."

She spread out her towel, took off her dress to reveal her blue bikini, carefully folded the dress, and set it down. Then she dragged the kayak out into the calm water, thick with seaweed, raising all sorts of yellowish bubbles around her and the craft.

"Get in," she ordered me.

I walked into the water. When she saw how difficult it was for me, she helped me climb in by holding my arm.

"Pick up the paddle. Show me how you hold it."

29.

I showed her and was immediately reprimanded. Lu turned out to be someone who enjoyed reprimanding, threatening and swearing but she was also encouraging and determined; she clearly enjoyed giving me lessons and wanted me to learn how to kayak. We stayed in the water for at least two hours, time that was measured with countless phrases of no, no, no! not like that, and other disparaging comments blurted out in the informal *tu*, which she then corrected to the more polite *lei* form, only to then go back to addressing me with *tu*, alternating encouraging phrases like go on, that's it, that's it! with things like: how in the hell did you manage to graduate from university? my illiterate grandfather is smarter than you, I can't believe you did that again! now why are you laughing? you're worse than Niní, I said keep your eye on the bow! keep it straight, no, you're not going to capsize, where do you think you're going—Ponza? I hadn't had so much fun in a long time, actually maybe only on one other occasion in my life, during a trip to the States with my fourth daughter, Chiara. It was about ten years ago, just the two of us; every morning we took the ferry from Williamsburg to Manhattan, with her criticizing my every step and word, and I just laughed and laughed, the same way I was doing with Lu.

At the end of the lesson she said that I showed promise and she ran off. But the following day—she was always very punctual, at half past one—she started berating my efforts even more rigorously than the day before. The sea had grown choppy overnight and no longer looked like a large, tepid morass. There was a hot wind, and the waves that broke on the shore were brown, their crests dirty with foam. Often they rolled in not one after the other, but side by side, crashing into each other and coming to blows, roaring angrily.

"Maybe we should skip the lesson today," I said.

"Get in, quit wasting my time," she said using the formal voice.

"Why don't you take the kayak out? That way I can watch and learn, it would be reassuring."

"No."

"Why?"

"Because then I'll want it."

"Want what?"

"The kayak."

"But I promised it to your son."

"I want it. Now."

"So take it."

She looked at me with resentment for a long moment. "Do you want to learn or talk nonsense? If you want to talk nonsense, I'm leaving."

It was harder to get into the boat than before because it kept tipping up and crashing into the waves that came bounding into the shore. And Lu issued her instructions so rapidly that I had a hard time understanding her, I just sat there holding the paddle and laughing. Upwind, Lu shouted, keep it upwind, you're taking on water, what's your problem? do you understand what I'm saying or not? what's the matter, are you scared? at your age what could possibly scare you? the water only comes up to my hips, see? I'm standing right here, it's this shallow, the beach is right there, this is insane! you call these waves? this is nothing, these are ruffles, and you know it, too, so paddle, paddle! But I just kept on laughing, randomly striking at the water with the paddle; I really was afraid, but I was also terribly amused by my stupid old-man fear, by the way the waves came slapping into me sideways, spraying water all over me, by how Lu swore with a strange accent from some small mountain village, by the image of me drowning two meters away from shore, me, the one who used to boast to Nina, Laura, Nora, and all my children and grandchildren about what a great swimmer I had been when I was young, I could have been a freestyle champion, I was fast and strong at swimming underwater, too, oh old age! It's so funny, Lu, so terribly funny.

But soon enough, she got fed up. She hoisted herself onto the kayak, straddled it, scooted up close behind me, put her hands over mine, and shouted let's go! in my right ear, leaning tensely and awkwardly into my back—go, go, come on, paddle hard now, go! Soon the kayak stopped taking on water, the bow sliced through the foamy crests, and I stopped laughing, I became all-absorbed in learning and listening to the words that popped into my mind, and I was happy: oh, what a sea monster we are together, Lu, a blend of polyethylenekevlar-oldflesh-sondaughter-sea-mother-lifedeath, much worse than the giant squid!, we're the mystical creature now. Then she was the one who started laughing at my rambling comments; she started to laugh; Lu, at my back, wild, a powerhouse of energy. This—I thought to myself—is how my mother must have been. But I never saw her like this, my father never saw her like this, maybe no one ever saw her like this, and so, never seeing herself reflected in others, maybe my mother never saw herself for who she truly was. We at home must have intuited that she was a knot that was difficult to loosen, my father for sure, and he was scared by it, and his fear must have caused me to be afraid. But thankfully, through the Lu of today, through the Lu that pressed up against the tough old skin of my back, through the Lu that I couldn't see, my mother was breaking free, disrupting the order of time, she was part of the future, I was in the distant past, she had so much life to live, I was at the end of mine, she was fleeing with apparent and destructive joy, I was stable—unstable—my shoulders burdened with her unexpressed burden.

When we passed the breakers and reached deeper waters, Lu slipped off the kayak with an intense cry of pleasure, dove down deep, and reappeared on the other side of the boat.

"Now paddle back to the shore on your own," she said cheerfully.

"What if I can't?"

She smiled wildly, her white teeth contrasting sharply with her dark skin. "You're a dangerous old man, you know that? I need to watch out with you, one moment you're all trembly, the next minute you're a wild man. Go on, paddle, you'll be on the shore in a few seconds, you'll fly."

She swam behind me and the kayak truly did obey the paddle, the keel sliding gently over the top of the waves.

Day after day, I improved. Eventually Lu stopped scolding me and went back to talking to me with her usual *lei* form. A couple of times she even took her old red canoe out and we paddled side by side to the pier and back, chatting about this and that.

"I heard you were a good student."

"Only according to Maurizio, the other teachers thought I was normal."

"Evelina says you know three or four languages."

"And yet I never manage to say anything intelligent in any of them."

"That happens to most people."

"To me more often."

Stuff like that. One afternoon—she was about to leave, she was wearing a red sundress and had already put on her backpack—she said, "One of these days, I have to ask you a question. And I want you to tell me the truth."

"I don't know if I can do that."

"You're a worldly man, I'm sure you can."

"Fine, but then ask me now; never put things off."

"No, today I don't feel like it."

"Why?"

"Because I'm happy."

And off she went.

30.

The following day she showed up looking serious. She was wearing jean shorts and a faded tank top. Her tone was aggressive from the start. "We're done."

"You don't have anything left to teach me?"

"No, for a man your age, the little you've learned is more than you'll ever need."

"I was hoping to become as good as a young man."

"An old man will never be like a young man."

"I don't agree. All you need to do is diminish the reality of the first term of comparison and reinforce the second with a little imagination."

"You say things that mean nothing."

She pushed the kayak into the water, told me to climb in, and then looked at me sourly. "To the pier and back."

"Alone?"

"Do you want to call Evelina?"

"I don't understand."

"It doesn't matter, I do. Now go."

"What if I drown?"

"Then you'll have spared yourself a little senile folly."

I got beyond the breakers with some ability and then, paddling hard, I followed the invisible diagonal line that ideally cut through the dark blue water and connected Lu to the dark tip of the pier. I stayed focused the whole way,

I didn't want to make a single mistake. I reached my destination drenched in sweat, with sore muscles, and pleased with myself. I was about to face the complex maneuver of turning around when I heard someone call my name: Nico.

It was Silvestro. He was standing in the sunlight, a solid mass, well-proportioned; I realized that he must have been ten years younger than Evelina. He was stepping into a green-black wetsuit but stopped when he caught sight of me, and he called to me from the tip of the pier. "That frumpy old-man hat ruins the aesthetics of the kayak."

"Sorry," I replied, "but the human factor is what it is."

"You're a funny guy, but we all know there's a serpent lurking deep inside you."

"There's a serpent inside everyone, that's where we come from. Humans descend less from Adam than from the serpent."

"But you, my dear sir, are more poisonous than other people, so watch out: I keep a gun by my bed, and if you ever try to mess around with my wife again, I'll kill you."

"You'll have an easy time of it, I keep nothing by my bed. Bye, see you around."

I was pleased with myself for maintaining a steady voice and casual tone. I started the maneuver to turn the kayak around but, as I was a bit nervous, it didn't come out as well as I had hoped. Gradually I calmed down, put the incident with Silvestro aside and—breathing heavily, my hat firmly on my head—I crossed the deep water and followed the fine line back to the beach. One stroke on the right, followed by one on the left, I was paying such close attention to how the blades were entering the water and was so empty of other thoughts that the loud rumble behind me that sounded like an object crashing into and slapping the surface of the water—a loud roar punctuated by a steady doom-doom—was late in reaching my brain, as if the trumpet heralding the apocalypse was broken.

I twisted around the little that I could and saw a large white cloud of water rumbling across the dark blue sea towards me. I grew even more scared when I noticed an oblong shadow inside the cloud, it was almost on top of me, it was going to crush me. How stupid it is to be afraid of such things in my old age; all the work I've done to not fear for my life has been for naught. Then the sea cloud and slivers of light came into focus: it was a jet ski, it was going to crash into me. Fortunately, the person at the wheel veered sharply just in time. Then the jet ski came up alongside me, sprayed me with a wall of water, and zipped off, attempted to buck the waves, turned around and came straight back at me, the kayak rocking hard from the waves it had caused.

That's when I realized that sitting at the wheel of the powerful machine that smelled of gasoline was Silvestro, in his green-black wetsuit.

"Scared you, huh?" he yelled at me with excitement, bobbing on the waves.

"A little."

"Nothing to be afraid of, this machine is amazing. It's so light, the body's made of Polytex. Barely uses any gas at all. If you really want to impress your grandkids, this is the ticket. Sure, it's a couple years old, but it's in perfect condition; I can sell it to you—special price—for nine thousand euro."

"Thanks but I'm not very good with powerful machines, not on land, or on water."

"Sure, you old swine," he said. "Take my advice. Even a decrepit geezer like you would look good on one of these.

They make you feel young again, I'll give it to you for eight thousand. You've got the money, there could be a war, a virus, a real estate bubble, the Africans might invade and then money would mean zilch. Spend what you've got, enjoy the little time you have left. Let me know."

And off he went towards the pier—roar doom, roar doom—and in a matter of seconds he went back to being a cloud of water.

31.

Once he was gone, everything, and I mean absolutely everything, took on far more realistic tones. I was frozen through and the boat was full of water, but the effort it took to paddle warmed me up. When I got to the breakers, I handled the kayak pretty well and I reached my destination flying from crest to crest. I hoped that Lu was watching me, that she would say well done, but I don't think she glanced at me once; she was sitting on the towel, smoking and talking on her cell phone. She didn't even help me drag the kayak up onto the beach, I did it by myself, panting with fatigue, and then quickly put on my robe.

From the warmth in her voice and how she laughed, it was clear she was talking to Gino. When she finished, she said happily and with the informal *tu*, "You took too long."

I sat down on the sand next to her. "It's not a short trip, there and back."

"Even so, you still took too long."

"I ran into a problem. Silvestro practically crashed into me on his jet ski."

"He's out of his head these days."

"Yes, I noticed."

"All your fault."

"Could be."

"Did he mention me?"

"No."

"He's torturing me."

"Why?"

"I took something that Evelina gave him thirty years ago and now he wants it back."

"Give it back to him."

"I threw it away."

"Why?"

"I was angry."

"So what are you going to do?"

"I guess I'll have to run away. I'm going to Venice with Gino and Niní in two weeks, never coming back."

"Brava."

"In Venice I'll wear all the chic clothes you bought me."

"I'm glad."

"I hope it rains, I'm even bringing the trench coat."

"Great."

Her face clouded over. "You're teasing me. But I get it, you're right, I'm rustic. See those mountains? I come from a town up there. I wanted to make something of myself and look where I ended up. But I won't stay here forever, I'm determined not to, and I know what I need to do."

"I don't want to know."

"You sure?"

"Let's just sit here like this."

"Like this how?"

"With me younger than your son, and you considering me older and stupider than your grandfather."

"Can I at least ask you my question?"

"I warned you that I have no wisdom to share."

"I heard you, but I want to ask you just the same."

"Fine."

She glanced towards the pier. "When does desire end?"

"Are you tired of feeling desire?"

"Yes. I want to quit running from one thing to the next, it makes me feel stupid and cruel. Whenever I try to obtain what I feel like I'm missing, I always end up giving others what they need first."

"How old are you?"

"Twenty-four."

"It takes time, and not to stop desiring, but for the intensity to fade."

"I want it to stop now. What do I need to do?"

"I don't know, I told you I'm not wise."

She shrugs and narrows her eyes at me. Then she nods in the direction of the kayak and grins maliciously. "Can I take it out?"

"Why do you feel the need to ask?"

"I just do."

"Why?"

"So I can hear you say no," she says pretending not to care.

I looked out to sea.

"Go on."

She jumped to her feet with a whoop of joy, set her cell phone down on the towel, and ran to the kayak. She was all muscles and nerves, and in a matter of minutes the craft was a dark black spot on the purple sea.

I walked home, retrieved the gift that Evelina had given to Silvestro thirty years ago and returned to the beach with the money clip in the pocket of my robe. I went back to reading the *Toilers of the Sea*, but on Lu's towel. When she came back, she laughed and said I looked like a monk trying to memorize the bible, and then went on to praise the keel of the boat. I had no idea what possible merits the keel might have had but I listened all the same. When she finished, I started to get up, groaning as usual with the effort, and while I was doing so, I suddenly felt dizzy and almost fell over, but she grabbed my hand.

"Are you alright?"

"Fine." I handed her the money clip. "Is this the object you lost?"

She took it with disbelief. I was moved to see how surprised she was.

"Did Maurizio give it to you?"

"I found it in the sand, just a few minutes ago."

She burst out laughing. "No, but really, who are you? I'm not afraid of anyone or anything but you're actually beginning to frighten me."

Her words made me happy. They were more or less the same ones my mother said to me a few weeks before dying, in the hospital, when to prove to her that I was special, I read her a short story of mine that a magazine had recently published.

32.

Today is Sunday, the weather's nice, there's even something of a cool breeze that may blow away some of this humidity, which is entirely atypical for the autumn. I slept well, deeply, but in the early hours of the morning when I went to the bathroom, a sudden sharp pain twisted through my spine, extending like blades to both sides, grabbing hold of my inner organs and lacerating them for a few long moments, taking away even the strength to cry out. Now I'm back on the beach, writing to calm down, but every so often I have to reach up and hold onto my hat with one hand, and when I do that, the pages in my notebook flutter and crash into each other with small slapping sounds.

I've discovered that while Sunday, for me, is just another day, here it's a day for outings, with cars blasting music from their windows, parking in long rows along the beachfront as if it were summer, loud adult voices, children shouting and crying, all of which brings life back to the dunes, the beach, the sea. Tourists and holiday-makers are practically all gone, these are local families and day-trippers from nearby towns. Some of them set up umbrellas and lounge chairs, they bring coolers and containers of home-cooked food. But the majority of them stroll up and down the shore, some in their Sunday clothes, carrying their shoes and walking barefoot, others in their bathing suits.

Although they walk by me, they feel far away; everything seems distant today. Around eleven o'clock I look up and, beyond the veil of my cataracts, I see Maurizio. While I can't quite tell if he's dressed in his Sunday best, I see that he's wearing a red shirt and blue short pants, which I like to imagine clean. He's with Niní, who is in his bathing suit; the boy stops to pick up something, he dawdles, his father waits. When they walk by me, I say hello, but Maurizio pretends not to hear me and keeps walking. When the kid turns back to look in my direction, his father grabs his arm, as if a treacherous ditch separated us.

I feel sorry for myself, I try to think about something

else. An elegantly dressed Indian man approaches and politely tries to sell me some jewelry that he keeps in a leather pouch. A young couple pushes a stroller with an infant in it across the wet sand, it's hard-going, they're tired, they quarrel. From out of the tunnel in the scrub brush come Gino and Lu, they drag the red canoe up to the water but don't use it right away. They strip down to their bathing suits and start to play beach tennis on the dry sand not far away from me.

I concentrate on them. Lu hits the ball hard and Gino struggles to respond, he has to move farther and farther back on the sand until he bumps into my kayak, he waves to me in apology, embarrassed, as if he'd bumped into me. Lu acknowledges me with a quick wave, I wave back cheerfully, and she calls out to her boyfriend to keep playing. She's resolved in her movements, darting quickly from side to side, growing larger with each lunge or leap.

Now, it's almost midday, and the presence of women, teenagers, and children has increased, there are surely more of them than men. The mood is growing livelier, there's the sound of laughter, people calling to one another, a kind of cheerfulness that draws me in, like when I see people dancing, that makes me, even though I'm old, even though I don't know how to dance, want to throw myself into the fray with extravagant moves. But then, Sibilla and Dr. Martano come up behind me; Sibilla even removes my hat and runs her hands through my hair with an excess of intimacy. What a pleasure, I say, and get to my feet. Before someone again mentions an invitation, I invite them over to my house one evening, all of them, and Sibilla exclaims: great, that way we can braid your hair like when you were at nursery school and cried. Dr. Martano doesn't seem interested in either dinner or braiding my hair, but when she notices Maurizio and the boy who happen to walk by in that very moment, she caustically says: it's incredible how much Niní resembles his father, if only we knew who he was. Then she giggles and adds, looking at me: Melania says that you understand everything but pretend not to know anything: can you tell us something about that poor child's father? It's me, I say, Niní looks just like I did when I was seven years old and deeply unhappy; if you'd like I can show you a photo I have on my computer. Sibilla and Dr. Martano smile with hesitation, either they didn't get my joke or they found it in poor taste.

Suddenly everyone on the beach is focused on something happening on the pier. A terrifyingly loud sound makes its way across the water, it's Silvestro, showing off his jet ski. The closer he gets, the faster a group of people—five or six boys, a few men, and women who are his friends or lovers, including Sibilla and Dr. Martano, who smugly exclaim with disgust, what a ruckus the idiot is making—make their way over to the spot on the beach where it looks like he will land.

Even Lu. She stops playing, throws her racket down on the sand, and hurries over to the small crowd welcoming Silvestro, dressed in a red wetsuit for the occasion. Maurizio stops a few steps away, looks at Silvestro and then out to sea; clearly he doesn't want to have anything further to do with me. This saddens me, I've grown attached to the heavy yet nimble man, and wish we could just be simple friends. Niní, who's standing by his father's side, suddenly deserts him—Maurizio doesn't even try to hold him back—and jumps across the imaginary ditch and over to my side.

He points to the group of people who surround the now immobile jet ski. "Did you see the giant squid?"

"It's just a machine."

My comment disappoints him, he feels betrayed, and it gets worse when Silvestro starts up the jet ski and revs the engine noisily.

"You hear how ugly it is?"

"The giant squid doesn't make all that noise."

"Yes, it does, and I hate it."

"It makes a noise, but a different kind. And anyway, it's important to learn not to hate anyone."

When the jet ski departs, Niní and I both realize with sudden disappointment that of all the women who'd been hoping to hold onto Silvestro and ride the Sunday waves, Lu had prevailed. She waves to Gino and he waves back. Her perfect teeth shine, she holds on tightly to Evelina's husband and off they go.

"I'm going to follow the giant squid," Niní says darkly. "And kill it."

I reach out my hand to shake his. "Good luck," I say.

He shakes mine back. "My palms are sweaty," he says softly.

"Everybody's hands get a little sweaty at times."

He runs off, ignoring Maurizio, who calls out to him. I sigh. Writing about what really happens is pointless; actually, precisely because these notes are so clear, they risk disrupting things. At times like this, it's better to read, so I read and read until there's a sudden gust of wind, oh! I cry out in disappointment, almost falling over in my chair, as my hat gets blown away.

I reach out to catch it—triggering a sharp pain in my neck—but it flies off impossibly fast. I try to stand up but remain doubled over, the wind gusts come even harder, people's clothes get glued to their bodies, people in bathing suits who were walking in ankle-deep water run up onto dry land chased by the waves, the two or three umbrellas that had been planted in the sand fly away faster than my hat, the sky turns black, it bears down with all its weight on a squirt of white lead paint that rests on the suddenly stormy sea.

I stand up straight with a long painful rale and see Niní in my kayak, he's struggling with the oversize paddle out in high waves. He's desperately trying to chase Silvestro and his mother, that little figurine outlined in gold that has definitively escaped from my decaying body. It's pointless—I think—to try and write anymore, just stop. Even my most personal motivation has worn thin. Meanwhile I fight my way through the tangled knot of wind and other objects in an effort to reach the old red canoe and push it into the water, to end well and bring the boy home safe, as I feel responsible for him. In the fictional version, I know exactly what to do: I fix this, tweak that, this is the first time in my life that I lean into a happy ending, I don't want someone to die. But in real life, there's little to be done, the situation is bad, now and then someone has to die, and we just have to learn to accept it.

33.

A purple worm descends from the heavens twisting and spinning like a top across the surface of the water towards the jet ski, the kayak, the beach. Wind and rain beat down on the sea, the greenhouses, the houses on the dunes, ripping branches off willow trees, peeling the bark off eucalyptus trees, shredding the laurel bushes, sea pines, sick palm trees, confusing the words in my head. While sand, bits of rusty fence, women's dresses, and various lost articles fly up, I instinctively grasp onto the truest and most solid fact that comes to mind, so as not to be swept away by exaggerated descriptions. One month ago—I say to myself, and gradually my calm returns even as the storm continues to cut through sea and time—one month ago, after almost a decade of not bothering with my health, I decided to get a check-up, some blood work, a urine test. Not that I felt the need. I think I've made it clear that I can tolerate the ailments of old age: one day everything hurts, the next I feel great, why bother looking into it. Despite nothing being especially wrong—except my big toenail on my right foot, which was turning black and hurts—I started to feel slightly ashamed of my body, how audaciously alive it was. So I said to myself: let's see, and I went to the doctor.

The doctor saw me immediately, but he was in a foul mood. For someone who has to deal with so much misfortune, for someone who regularly sees tortured and afflicted young bodies, perhaps visiting an eighty-year-old whose only concern is a blackened toe nail is offensive; too lucky, too arrogant, too chatty, too everything. He examined me with a scowl, and he scowled as he wrote out a prescription for blood work, urine tests, and an antifungal cream for my nail.

I returned the following week with pages of percentages of red blood cells, white blood cells, cholesterol levels, triglyceride levels, enzymes, creatine, and other threatening words. The doctor glanced at the papers, crankier and unhappier than ever.

Then he looked down, his eyelids heavy. "You, my dear sir, are not well," he said.

I was silent.

"Do you know that the results indicate that you might have pancreatic cancer?"

I remained silent.

"Although I should say that I've never seen a cancer patient with such a good ESR. It may be pancreatitis."

I still didn't say anything.

"You'll need to do some more blood work right away."

I broke my silence. "Why?"

"What do you mean why? You did some blood tests, now you have to do others."

"I'm eighty-two years old."

"So?"

"Can you cure pancreatitis?"

"Umm . . . "

"What about pancreatic cancer?"

"Umm . . . "

"So why bother doing more blood work?"

"So we can formulate a diagnosis."

"I don't give a fuck about a diagnosis."

He was silent for a moment and then spoke up. "What about the abnormal blood tests? What about when the illness gets worse? What about when you're in terrible pain, or close to dying?"

"I don't have any symptoms for now."

"What about tomorrow?"

"If I start having them, I'll get used to them."

He struck me down like lightning. "The fuck you will."

I addressed him coldly. "Would you kindly look at my toenail again? That antifungal medicine didn't help at all. It's only getting blacker."

He started writing, the expression on his face suddenly

contrite. "Don't be foolish; your toenail is nothing. Do the blood tests immediately."

Me, foolish? My toenail, nothing?

So I rented this house by the sea.

About the Author

Domenico Starnone is the author of fifteen best-selling works of fiction, including: *Ties*, a *New York Times* Editors Pick and Notable Book of the Year, and a *Sunday Times* and *Kirkus Reviews* Best Book of the Year; *Trick,* a Finalist for the 2018 National Book Award and the 2019 PEN Translation Prize; and, *Trust*, "a short, sharp novel that cuts like a scalpel to the core of its characters" (*LA Times*). All three of these novels were translated by Pulitzer Prize-winner, Jhumpa Lahiri. In 2023, Europa Editions released an older title of Starnone's in a translation by Oonagh Stransky, the Strega Prize-winning *House on Via Gemito*, which was named a *Washington Post* and *Kirkus Reviews* Best Book of the Year and *New York Times* Editor's Choice. *The Mortal and Immortal Life of the Girl from Milan*, published in 2024, was described as "wonderfully off-kilter" by the *New Yorker*. Starnone is the recipient of all three of Italy's major literary prizes: The Strega prize, the Napoli prize, and the Campiello prize. His stories have appeared *The Paris Review*, *The Georgia Review*, and the *New Yorker*. Starnone was born in 1943 in Naples and currently lives in Rome.